Possessions and Exorcisms

Other titles in *The Mysterious & Unknown* series:

The Mysterious & Unknown

Possessions and Exorcisms

by Adam Woog

ReferencePoint Press®

San Diego, CA

©2013 ReferencePoint Press, Inc.
Printed in the United States

For more information, contact:
ReferencePoint Press, Inc.
PO Box 27779
San Diego, CA 92198
www.ReferencePointPress.com

Acknowledgments
My thanks to Karen Kent and Jody Bower for their contributions.—AW

LIBRARY OF CONGRESS CATALOGING-IN-PUBLICATION DATA

Woog, Adam, 1953–
    Possessions and exorcisms / by Adam Woog.
      p. cm. -- (The mysterious & unknown)
    Includes bibliographical references and index.
    ISBN 978-1-60152-474-4 (hardback) -- ISBN 1-60152-474-9 (hardback)
    1. Demoniac possession. 2. Demonology. 3. Spirit possession. 4. Exorcism. I. Title.
    BF1555.W66   2013
    133.4'26--dc23
                                                                                2012003929

CONTENTS

FOREWORD

"Strange is our situation here upon earth."
—*Albert Einstein*

Since the beginning of recorded history, people have been perplexed, fascinated, and even terrified by events that defy explanation. While science has demystified many of these events, such as volcanic eruptions and lunar eclipses, some remain outside the scope of the provable. Do UFOs exist? Are people abducted by aliens? Can some people see into the future? These questions and many more continue to puzzle, intrigue, and confound despite the enormous advances of modern science and technology.

It is these questions, phenomena, and oddities that Reference-Point Press's *The Mysterious & Unknown* series is committed to exploring. Each volume examines historical and anecdotal evidence as well as the most recent theories surrounding the topic in debate. Fascinating primary source quotes from scientists, experts, and eyewitnesses as well as in-depth sidebars further inform the text. Full-color illustrations and photos add to each book's visual appeal. Finally, source notes, a bibliography, and a thorough index provide further reference and research support. Whether for research or the curious reader, *The Mysterious & Unknown* series is certain to satisfy those fascinated by the unexplained.

INTRODUCTION

Inhabited by Spirits

S ince the beginning of time, people have tried to explain the unexplainable. In the case of a person who acts bizarrely or becomes ill for no apparent reason, the cause is sometimes a mystery. Many cultures and religions believe that one explanation for such mysteries is the existence of evil spirits.

According to this belief, a supernatural demon can occupy, or possess, a person's body. This gives the evil spirit the power to control the person. Some spirits are said to be just mischievous, but others cause sickness, madness, misfortune, or even death. Furthermore, some cultures believe that evil spirits can possess animals and inanimate things like houses and trees.

A Battle with Evil

A culture's belief in demonic possession has always been closely entwined with its religious faiths. Most observers agree that the reasons for a belief in possession are varied, but religion is always a factor. Jody Bower, a scholar of cultural mythology, notes, "Whatever the psychological or cultural needs that underlie the phenomenon of possession, it is first and foremost a religious experience."[1]

Different terms for demonic possession are used in various cultures and religions, but the basic idea is the same: The phenomenon is part of a fundamental, eternal, and never-ending struggle between good and evil. On one side is God (or several gods). On the other is the devil—the very figure of wickedness, also called Satan—or a larger group of evil spirits.

Belief in this conflict has developed and changed in countless ways throughout history. In all cases, however, it remains an attempt to explain those mysteries that seem to defy explanation. Writer Matt Baglio comments, "The idea of the Devil has evolved over time, primarily as a way to explain the existence of evil in a world created by an all-powerful and loving God."[2]

Different Ideas

The details of belief in possession vary widely, depending on the religion or culture. In some cases the evil spirits are assumed to be ghosts of dead people who are angry or upset. Depending on the culture, demons can also take a variety of shapes and forms. For example, some cultures believe that evil spirits can change shape and appear as humans or animals. Others believe that demons are invisible or have characteristics such as terrifying eyes or sharp claws.

Most who believe in the possibility of demonic possession also believe that those demons can be driven out, or exorcised. This is true in Catholicism, Protestantism, Judaism, Islam, Hinduism, Buddhism, and their various subgroups. But it is also true in virtually all other religions and cultures, particularly the many shamanic religions around the world. (Shamanic or shamanistic religions emphasize communication with the spirit world.)

Sometimes these religions' exorcism rituals are relatively calm. They might consist mostly of prayer and dialogue between the

HRISTUS EIICIT DÆMONIUM MUTUU ET IMPERAT IMPURIS SPIRITIB,.⁵³

Lucæ Cap. XI.

cit o misero Dominus Cacodæmona Muto | Spiritibus Chriftus stygiis dominatur, et illos
Protinus obsefsus verba diserta sonat. | Cogit ad imperium cedere sede sua.
erunt inv. et del. Gabriel Bodenear fecit. Negot. Acad. Cæs. Franc. excud. Aug. Vind. Cum Grat. et Priv. S. C. Maj.

exorcist and the possessed person. However, sometimes they are highly emotional and dramatic. For example, the exorcism rituals in many shamanistic religions involve a shaman going into a trance in order to contact the demon. Similarly, the afflicted person might behave even more strangely during or after the ritual than before it. On occasion, an exorcist might beat the possessed person or inflict worse punishment in the belief that this will drive the demon out.

Links to Mental Illness

A great many religions teach that possession is real—but also that it is rare. For example, the Christian, Islamic, and Jewish faiths generally acknowledge the existence of possession-like symp-

Onlookers marvel as Jesus drives a demon out of a possessed man. All of the world's major religions believe it is possible for spirits to possess and to be exorcised from human beings.

A great many
religions teach
that possession
is real—but also
that it is rare.

toms. However, these religions are also careful to point out that most cases are, in fact, due to mental illness or a brain disorder. Long ago, people who had epilepsy, a brain disorder that causes seizures, or schizophrenia, a mental illness that typically causes hallucinations (seeing things that are not there) or delusions (false beliefs, such as hearing voices that other people cannot hear), were thought to be possessed rather than experiencing symptoms of an illness. Baglio comments, "You can't deny the fact that many illnesses in the past were misunderstood. [A] church has to be very careful about confusing mental illness with demonic possession."[3]

The majority of physicians, psychiatrists, and other mental health professionals agree with this assertion. However, a few mental health professionals and clergy think that exorcism may serve a useful psychological purpose. They suggest that rituals associated with exorcisms can help mentally ill people who believe that they are possessed. *Time* magazine writer Gilbert Cruz comments, "While many health care workers view [exorcisms] with suspicion, some doctors believe exorcism could help cure certain mental illnesses."[4]

Fascination with Exorcism

In ancient times, especially among some shamanistic cultures, demonic possession and exorcism were not rare. They were commonplace and important occurrences in people's lives. In Western culture, however, they fell into relative obscurity for several centuries.

That has changed, however, and in recent decades there has been a resurgence of interest in possessions and exorcisms. This attention was sparked in 1974 by a popular movie, *The Exorcist*. The public's fascination with the subject has also been fueled by other trends. Among these are a surge in interest and research into paranormal activity and a growing interest in spirituality.

The existence of Christian sects that emphasize exorcism have added to this growing interest. By several estimates there are hundreds of sects in the United States alone that believe that exorcism is needed to drive out demons and maintain spiritual health. Sometimes these groups' exorcisms are as quiet as private counseling sessions. Other times they are highly public and boisterous rituals, and these well-publicized events have been particularly effective in arousing public interest. Writer Paul Burnell asserts, "In a world where Satanists appear on prime-time TV, neo-pagan religions gather vast followings and tarot [mystic] card readings are available in the newspapers, experts say it's no surprise that the number of exorcisms worldwide is rising."[5]

The symptoms of these cases of alleged demonic possession and exorcism are, in many ways, typified by one incident. This is the strange tale of a teenager named Anneliese Michel. Her story is a famous example of what possession and exorcism are all about.

CHAPTER 1

In the Grip of Demons: The Possessed

Born in 1952 and growing up in the town of Klingenberg am Main, Germany, Anneliese Michel seemed like a normal kid. Anneliese's family also seemed normal. Her father, Josef, ran a sawmill or was a carpenter (accounts vary); her mother, Anna, kept house; and she had three or four sisters (again, sources vary). Like a lot of their neighbors, the Michels were devout Catholics—although Anneliese was perhaps even more so. All in all, the Michels were an ordinary family, with nothing in their lives to give anyone reason to suspect that bizarre events would soon overtake them.

Strange Symptoms

The strange events started in the late 1960s, when Anneliese was a teenager. She began to have blackouts and convulsions. These frightening episodes left her weak and confused, and she had no memory of them afterward. For a few years, the incidents happened only once in a while. Doctors told Anneliese and her parents that in many cases such symptoms bother people in childhood but go away when they become adults. So her family was concerned but not panicked.

Then much worse things started happening. The convulsions and blackouts grew more frequent and stronger. She also began to have visions of a horrible demon with horns and a bizarre, revolting face. She told people it loomed over her while she was praying. The presence of the demon made her reluctant to keep praying, in case it reappeared, but she continued to do so.

Anneliese's behavior became even more erratic, when, as a teen, she joined a group making a religious pilgrimage to a sacred shrine in Italy. One of the women in the group noticed that Anneliese avoided walking past a religious image and refused to drink water from a holy spring. The woman also noticed that Anneliese smelled astonishingly bad. Furthermore, Anneliese sometimes complained that she herself smelled something terrible, though no one else could smell it.

The situation grew worse after Anneliese returned home. She saw more visions of wicked faces telling her to abandon God. She sensed the terrible stench more often and became increasingly disturbed whenever she was near priests, churches, or religious images. As if this were not enough, Anneliese started going into trances, during which she spoke in a voice that was unlike her normal voice. It was deep and rough, and it cruelly mocked her and everyone around her.

During these trances Anneliese sometimes became physically violent. She destroyed furniture and household objects, and she tried to hit anyone who attempted to help her. According to some sources, she ran around the house as though she were an animal, and her body swelled up in strange places. Sometimes she tore off her clothes because she became so hot, and the next moment she began to shiver and complain that she was freezing. But then the disturbing experiences seemed to go away as mysteriously as they had appeared.

Behavior Grows More Bizarre

Thinking she might be getting better, Anneliese's parents let her go to college in a nearby city after she graduated from high school. She took classes to become a teacher and did seem to be getting better. She felt stable enough to begin dating another student, who became her boyfriend. But Anneliese's break from strange behavior did not last for long. While at school she started having episodes of paralysis. She became violent toward her boyfriend and any others who tried to get near her. And she began to go into trances again.

"I'm afraid."
—Anneliese Michel, just before her death.

Anneliese also became more extreme in her religious devotion. For example, she denied herself comfort in various ways. One way she did this was to sleep on a bare stone floor every night. Anneliese deprived herself of comfort because she believed that it would help other people she thought were sinners—that is, people who did wicked things. She thought that she could help these sinners become better people. She was especially concerned with the many young people who were drug addicts or lived on the streets. She also thought that she could help "wayward" priests who did not, in her opinion, follow traditional Catholic teachings strictly enough.

Anneliese's behavior worsened after she lost her grandmother and one or both of her sisters (accounts vary). She wept uncontrollably and screamed for no reason. She developed wounds that bled spontaneously. And she quit eating almost completely, in the belief that fasting would help her. Her body continued to go through rapid changes in temperature, and at times she still suffered temporary paralysis or trembled violently. On occasion she was unable to walk, and she frequently saw visions of her dead relatives. Hallucinations continued to plague her, as did voices telling her that she was damned and fated to go to hell.

According to some accounts, Anneliese experienced even stranger symptoms than these. There were reports that she occasionally ate bizarre things, like flies, spiders, and coal, and that she sometimes licked her own urine off the floor. She supposedly bit the head off a dead bird, and she allegedly climbed under a table, where she stayed for two days, barking like a dog.

Furthermore, Anneliese claimed that she did not have just one evil spirit inside her. She said there were seven. Among them were Adolf Hitler, the Emperor Nero (a cruel ruler in ancient Rome), and the devil himself. Anneliese also said that the spirit of a priest named Valentin Fleischman was inside her. According to several sources, Fleischmann was a wicked German priest who was convicted of committing assault, murder, and other crimes in the sixteenth century.

Doctors at a psychiatric clinic examined Anneliese while she was still enrolled in college. They diagnosed grand mal epilepsy, a medical condition that causes strong convulsions. The doctors felt that her illness was made worse by mental disorders, including schizophrenia. Anneliese agreed to follow their advice and undergo psychiatric and medical treatment. This included medication to control her epilepsy and stabilize her other disorders as

Did You Know?

Anneliese Michel supposedly had 67 exorcism sessions before she died.

much as possible. The treatment went on for several years, but it did not seem to help. So her increasingly desperate parents decided to abandon the advice of conventional medical doctors.

The Exorcism Begins

The distressed family begged the church to perform an exorcism to drive the evil spirit away. But the church takes the ritual of

Anneliese Michel underwent numerous exorcisms in hopes of freeing herself from her demons. Between her many disturbing visions were a few that Anneliese described as more positive. In one such vision, she said, the Virgin Mary (pictured) urged her to be brave.

exorcism very seriously. The Catholic Church teaches that people who believe they are possessed by demons more often suffer from some sort of mental illness. Because of this, church officials might study a case of suspected possession for years before agreeing to perform an exorcism—and even then rarely authorize the procedure.

For several years the church refused to grant an exorcism to Anneliese. It accepted the diagnosis of mental illness that the doctors had suggested. But Anneliese's parents persisted, and in 1975 church authorities agreed to the exorcism. Two church officials conducted the ritual, and a few family members and friends also were present. By this time Anneliese was so emaciated from not eating that she looked like a skeleton. She was so weak that she could not get out of bed.

As the priests recited prayers and brought out holy water and other sacred objects, Anneliese went into a trance. She shouted obscenities in her strange, deep voice and spat at the people around her. She became so agitated that she had to be held down by several people. But then the trance ended, and Anneliese lay back, exhausted and confused. She seemed to be a little better, and the priests decided that they had succeeded in forcing one demon to leave. However, they said, the other six within her refused to go away. More exorcisms would be required.

The Demons Win

From the fall of 1975 until the spring of 1976, Anneliese had one or more exorcism sessions every week. According to some sources, a total of 67 rituals were performed. Some of them lasted four hours. After each one, Anneliese was exhausted and had no memory of what had occurred.

But she continued to get a little better. In between the sessions,

The Possession of Robbie Mannheim

One of the most famous cases of possession in modern times is that of Robbie Mannheim. Mannheim (not his real name) was an only child who lived near Washington, DC. At age 13 Mannheim began to exhibit extraordinarily weird behavior that lasted for several months. Everywhere he went, people heard unexplained noises. People who knew him said that heavy pieces of furniture sometimes moved on their own, and vases and lamps flew around when Mannheim was present. At school one day, students and teachers reported, his desk moved around the room, banging into other desks.

As things grew stranger, religious leaders tried to exorcise Mannheim. During a total of 30 sessions, he was tied to a bed, but bizarre things still happened. Bruises, words, and other marks that he could not have made appeared on his skin. Mannheim freed his hands, tore out a bedspring, and used it to cut an exorcist so seriously that stitches were needed. The boy hit another priest and broke his nose. Furthermore, he spoke in a deep voice that was not his own and understood Latin, a language he did not know. But the exorcists apparently succeeded. As they performed the ceremony, the demons inside Mannheim left with a loud booming sound. Once that happened, the exorcists were able to stop their work. Mannheim felt at peace and was never troubled again.

Anneliese displayed almost no bizarre symptoms. Furthermore, she said that she often saw kindly or positive visions, including those of Jesus and the Virgin Mary (two important figures in her religion). Anneliese described a conversation in which the Virgin Mary told the teen that she had to be brave and fight the demons that possessed her.

By the spring of 1976, it seemed as though some of the demons had gone permanently. However, Anneliese felt the presence of one more spirit still remaining. It refused to show itself to the priests, instead making Anneliese continue to do bizarre things during her last exorcism sessions. For example, it apparently forced her to strip her clothes off and bang her head against a wall so hard that her teeth chipped. She also continued to violently attack people with so much strength that three men had to hold her down. Sometimes she had to be chained to a chair or to a bed.

Despite it all, Anneliese was still strongly devoted to God and believed that prayer would cure her. Over and over she stated that all of the demons would leave her and that soon all would be well. Some people have interpreted this last statement as indicating her belief that she would soon die. According to some sources, as part of her religious devotions during these last days, she knelt to pray so often that she seriously injured her knees. She tried to attend church with her parents, but she was so weak that they had to support her. She also vomited in church, which some observers have interpreted as the devil keeping her from taking communion, an important part of the Catholic ritual.

Anneliese continued to refuse food. Her health grew steadily worse, and her weight dropped to about 67 pounds (about 30kg). During what proved to be her final exorcism, Anneliese was too weak to kneel and pray without support from her parents. She died on July 1, 1976. According to some sources, that day was the exact day that she had earlier predicted as the moment when the last demon would leave and all would be well. Reportedly, her last words were to beg for absolution (a ritual cleansing of a person's sins) and to say to her mother, "I'm afraid."[6]

A Court Trial

Despite the failure of the exorcisms, the Michel family continued to believe that they and Anneliese had made the right decision. Anneliese's mother, Anna, said, "I know that we did the right thing because I saw the sign of Christ in her hands. She was bearing stigmata [wounds on her hands like those Christ suffered] and that was a sign from God that we should exorcise the demons. She died to save other lost souls, to atone [pay] for their sins."[7]

The possession of Anneliese Michel had for several years attracted international attention, and in particular her death was of concern to German authorities. They closely examined the details of the case to determine whether the Michels and the priests had committed a crime by allowing Anneliese to die. Government prosecutors spent more than two years sorting through the bizarre facts of the situation. German authorities brought the case to trial in 1978.

The government prosecutors who tried the case argued that Anneliese's parents, as well as the priests who had performed the exorcisms, were responsible for her death. According to the prosecution's expert witnesses, Anneliese could have lived if she had been hospitalized and force-fed. However, family members testified that this never would have happened; Anneliese had repeatedly refused to go into a hospital.

The prosecutors also accused the priests and Anneliese's parents of saying things that strengthened her belief that she was possessed. The government lawyers acknowledged that the Michels and the priests had not done this on purpose or with bad intent. Still, they said, the priests and her parents were guilty in part because their questions and statements affected Anneliese's already vulnerable and suggestible mind.

Meanwhile, the lawyers for Anneliese's parents and the priests argued that there was no law in Germany that prevented them from conducting an exorcism. They also pointed out the laws guaranteeing freedom of religion. Nonetheless, the four defendants were found guilty on two counts. One of these counts was failing to provide first aid to an ill person. This was a minor offense under German law. But the other count was more serious. This was negligent homicide—that is, allowing a death to occur, even if there was no intent to let the person die. The defendants were given suspended sentences (that is, they did not serve jail time), and they were ordered to pay the cost of the trial.

The Aftermath

Meanwhile, Anneliese had been buried in her hometown. In 1978, shortly after the trial concluded, her parents asked government authorities for permission to exhume their daughter's body. They wanted to do this because a nun had experienced a vision that Anneliese's body had not decayed in death, as would normally occur.

The Michels thought that the authorities would not allow them to dig up the body just because of this vision. So they stated that they wanted to dig their daughter up so that they could put her remains in a more expensive and elaborate coffin. The authorities agreed and gave the Michels permission. The result surprised only them: The body had decayed like any normal corpse.

Several years later, in 2005, the strange case of Anneliese

Michel came back into the public eye, when it inspired a highly fictionalized movie called *The Exorcism of Emily Rose*. It starred Jennifer Carpenter as Emily Rose (the movie's version of Anneliese). The movie, which is primarily about the trial following Emily's death, was a big hit.

Meanwhile, many people still visit Anneliese's grave. Many of these pilgrims come from far away. Some of them are coming for religious reasons. Others come because of a more general interest in supernatural events. Typically, they believe that Anneliese really did endure a horrible demonic possession, one that terrified her and everyone around her. Even though she did not succeed in fighting the powers of Satan, visitors believe, she is a heroine because she bravely fought against the evil spirit as long as she could.

The Stages of Possession

Anneliese Michel's life represents a bizarre—and possibly even an extreme case—of someone who either was possessed or thought she was possessed by demons. Much of what she experienced, however, can be found in her faith's views about possession. Catholicism officially recognizes three distinct stages of possession. Infestation is the point at which a demon first enters the victim's body. Oppression is the stage when the victim weakens and starts yielding and losing control to the evil spirit. And in full-blown possession, the demon tries to force the victim to commit terrible acts, such as murder or suicide. At this time, the victim's appearance and behavior change radically.

Anneliese's ordeal displayed most of the commonplace—and shocking—traits associated with a possessed person. For example, people who believe they are possessed by demons are (as she was) typically deeply religious. Suddenly becoming the opposite—that is, showing an aversion to religious objects—would clearly go against the normal pattern of behavior of those people. Many of Anneliese's symptoms are found in other reported cases of possession. One of the most typical of these, not surprisingly, is the sensation that a spirit or another personality is living inside one's body. Other symptoms described in accounts of possession (involving people other than Anneliese) include involuntary, violent, and/or bizarre behavior; unnatural strength; terrifying dreams, hallucinations, or visions; and screaming, especially of obscene or blasphemous words. Still another commonly reported symptom is speaking in a language that is unknown (either to the possessed person or, in some cases, to anyone). Convulsions, extreme physical pain, and suicidal thoughts are also often found.

A priest attempts to exorcise the demons that torment Emily Rose in a scene from the 2005 movie, **The Exorcism of Emily Rose.** *The movie brought Michel's tragic story back to life nearly 30 years after her death.*

What Possession Looks Like

Interpreting such symptoms as indicative of demonic possession has been common since ancient times. For example, a record of such behavior survives from the fourth century AD. Zeno of Verona was a Christian religious leader in what is now Italy. He wrote this graphic description of a person he believed to be possessed: "His face is suddenly deprived of colour, his body rises up of itself, the eyes in madness roll in their sockets and squint horribly, the teeth, covered with a horrible foam, grind between blue-white lips; and limbs twisted in all directions are given over to trembling; he sighs, he weeps."[8]

In the 1980s M. Scott Peck described his experiences researching exorcisms. Peck, who died in 2005, was a psychiatrist, as well as a deeply religious Christian and a best-selling writer. About his encounters with psychiatric patients who were apparently possessed, Peck recalled:

> When the [first victim] finally spoke clearly . . . an expression appeared on the patient's face that could be described only as Satanic. It was an incredibly contemptuous grin of utter hostile malevolence.
>
> [In the second case] the patient suddenly resembled a writhing snake of great strength, viciously attempting to bite the [exorcism] team members. More frightening than the writhing body, however, was the face. The eyes were hooded with lazy reptilian torpor—except when the reptile darted out in an attack, at which moment the eyes would open wide with blazing hatred.[9]

What Possession Feels Like

Sometimes, cases of apparent demonic possession have consequences that affect the possessed person more than they do other people. For example, people who are thought to be possessed often try to hurt themselves in various ways, such as by cutting themselves with knives or razor blades. Strange words can also appear on the skin, according to Adolf Rodewyk, a Catholic priest and writer:

> We have records of cases in which such skin writing developed within the sight of others present. These writings did not fade for weeks or months, so that fraud or artificial methods can be excluded. Those who observed these phenomena regarded them as surprising and odd, while the possessed experienced them as causes of intense pain, much as if burns or acid-caused injuries affected considerable portions of the skin.[10]

Similar symptoms have been seen in people of religions and cultures other than Catholicism. For example, 3 psychiatrists who studied possession cases in China in 1998 reported on a 40-year-old Buddhist farmer and mother of 5. This woman had been troubled by mysterious symptoms since her 20s. She told the psychiatrists that she was always tired and sometimes went into trances. During these she spoke nonsense words and had no control over or awareness of

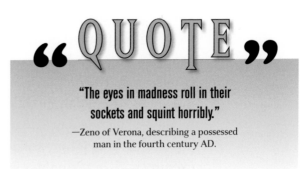

QUOTE

"The eyes in madness roll in their sockets and squint horribly."

—Zeno of Verona, describing a possessed man in the fourth century AD.

her behavior. At other times, she had difficulty concentrating and confused reality with fantasy. The woman added:

> I feel anxious, and sometimes my brain is in a turmoil, as if there is some prickly sensation all over my body. . . . I can't get to sleep at night because I seem to have seen something tiny and black before me. . . .
>
> The first attack was at dusk when the day's work was almost over. . . . As it was getting dark, I felt something like a cat running across my feet. I was scared and quickened my steps. . . .
>
> Later on, the catlike creature dashed right in front of me. I let out a cry, "I'm scared," and then lost my consciousness. I found myself in my house when I came to. Since then, I have suffered repeated attacks. My husband says that when I'm attacked I am possessed by different things, which I can hardly tell.[11]

When Possession Turns Deadly

There have been many reports of cases in which possessed people have confronted or attacked others. For example, the voices heard by supposedly possessed people might tell them that it is necessary to commit murder. One such example concerns a middle-aged woman in Oklahoma. She had no history of mental illness, personal problems, or drug or alcohol abuse. Then in 2001, according to one version of the story, the woman spent an evening with her daughter and two granddaughters. They experimented with a device called a Ouija board. This is a board that is said to allow people to communicate with the spirits of the dead. The story further relates that the woman and her family members succeeded in contacting one such spirit. However, later that night the spirit returned and possessed the woman. It told her to kill someone—anyone. The woman took a knife and fatally stabbed her son-in-law, who was sleeping in another room. She also tried to kill other members of her family. The woman then fled into the woods near her house, but a police search later found her. She had no memory of her murderous rampage. She was baffled by the incident but became convinced that it had been caused by her experimentation with the Ouija board.

Actions such as this are only some of the strange things that can happen during a possession. Some people say that the environment around the victim can also be damaged. According to some sources, during a possessed person's outbursts or during an exorcism, observers may be able to see, hear, and sense things like paint peeling off walls, strange noises, glasses of water starting to boil, furniture flying around the room, extreme changes in temperature, or strange odors.

What Causes Demonic Possession?

In the Oklahoma case the woman is thought to have inadvertently brought on her possession through her efforts to contact the spirit world. But this may be only one of the ways in which a person can become possessed. Some people believe that rejecting God and making a deal with the devil invites that evil demon in. The same outcome may occur when people perform black magic or take part in satanic cults.

Some people also believe that other kinds of blasphemous actions can make a person susceptible to possession. For example,

Most people who seek to contact spirits with the help of a Ouija board are just out to have fun. But at least one woman is convinced that her murderous rampage resulted from a spirit that possessed her during a Ouija board session.

in the opinion of some very conservative religious groups, a person can become vulnerable through exposure to violence or sex in the media. They believe that the same is true of such activities as using drugs, listening to aggressive music, or taking part in other things that are deemed dangerous or irreligious.

Although this is reported less frequently today than in centuries past, many cultures around the world believe a possession can occur when an evil person, such as a witch, sorcerer, or personal enemy, casts a curse or spell. These hexes can allegedly be cast in a number of ways. For example, a witch or sorcerer can use the evil eye on a person. An example of the evil eye's supposed power is a phenomenon called *vaskania*. Vaskania originated in ancient Greek folk beliefs. According to these legends, strangers, deformed people, people with blue eyes, and old women can have the evil eye. The evil eye harms anyone in its way by allowing evil spirits to possess people and cause sickness or bad fortune. Children and women are especially vulnerable.

The Greek Orthodox Church (a branch of the Christian religion) recognizes the existence of the evil eye. However, according to Sister Aimiliani, a nun at the Exaltation of the Holy Cross monastery in Thebes, Greece, the evil eye can affect only people who have negative thoughts in their hearts. She comments, "What one has to understand is that just as we recognise the existence of demons and the devil, we affirm that they have no more power than we give them. . . . If you face your own sins constantly, you will find both strength and humility, and the evil eye will not be able to affect you."[12]

Vaskania is only one example of the many ways in which demonic possession might be able to take hold. Depending on the specific culture or historical period, possession can be very different. In other words, every corner of the world has its own beliefs about demonic possession. The same is true for every time period in history.

CHAPTER 2

Possessions Throughout History and Across Cultures

Stories of evil spirits tormenting humans have been around since at least the beginning of recorded history and in every corner of the world. Writers Colin Blakemore and Sheila Jennett note, "The altered state of consciousness known as 'possession' has been, and remains, extraordinarily widespread in societies and cultures across the globe."[13]

The earliest known written accounts of the affliction are records carved in stone by the ancient Assyrians, who lived from about 1900 BC to 600 BC in what are now parts of Iraq, Iran, Syria, and Turkey. The Assyrians believed that dozens of demons lay in wait to attach themselves to humans. These spirits caused every physical and mental illness, and only prayer and sacrifice to the Assyrians' gods could cast the spirits out.

Dozens of other examples can be found in folk traditions that survive from ancient times. One comes from the Roma people (sometimes called Romany or Gypsies). According to their folklore, a demon called Mamioro appeared as an old, withered woman. She had the power to possess both people and places. Anthropologist Anne Sutherland comments, "Mamioro, a specific spirit who has become a disease carrier, causes illness simply by visiting the homes of Gypsies. Fortunately, she only visits dirty houses, so by keeping a clean house, the Gypsy can keep her away."[14]

Demonic Possession in the Bible

Demons are found not only in the ancient folk traditions of the world; they are also part of many modern religions. Of the world's major religions today, Christianity is the one that most prominently asserts the reality of possession. Christianity's holiest document is the Bible. In the Bible's New Testament, which is primarily dedicated to the story of Jesus Christ, more than 100 references to demonic possession appear. Many of these references can be found in the four main books known as the Gospels. John A. Hardon, a Catholic priest, comments, "There is almost no limit to the number and variety of diabolical possessions recorded in the Gospels alone. The victims of the devil were sometimes deprived of sight and speech. . . . At other times the victims lost only their speech. [Sometimes] the victims . . . were afflicted by the devil without being specified just how."[15]

Stories of Jesus casting out demons appear throughout the Gospels. Biblical scholars estimate that about one-quarter of the healings Jesus performed were full exorcisms. On one such occasion, the Bible states, Jesus cast out several thousand demons from a single person. Another notable biblical example is the story of a man who brought his son to Jesus. The boy had been seriously troubled since he was very young. He could not speak. He suffered convulsions, foamed at the mouth, gnashed his teeth, and became rigid. Furthermore, he sometimes tried to commit suicide by jumping into fire or water. But the boy was cured when Jesus commanded the evil spirit to leave.

Satan Takes Many Forms

During the Middle Ages and the Renaissance (roughly AD 450 to 1700), Religion was the dominant influence across Europe. A major part of religion—and thus daily life—revolved around the church's belief in the struggle between God and the devil. According to British historian Darren Oldridge, "The phenomena of demonic possession and exorcism occupied a central position in early modern religious thought."[16]

According to church teachings, God sometimes allowed Satan to test a person's religious strength. He let the demon enter that person's body, causing the victim to violently reject God. Overcoming the devil required tremendous bravery. A sixteenth-century religious scholar, Johann Weaver, commented, "Satan possesses a great courage, incredible cunning, superhuman wisdom . . . and infinite hatred towards the human race."[17]

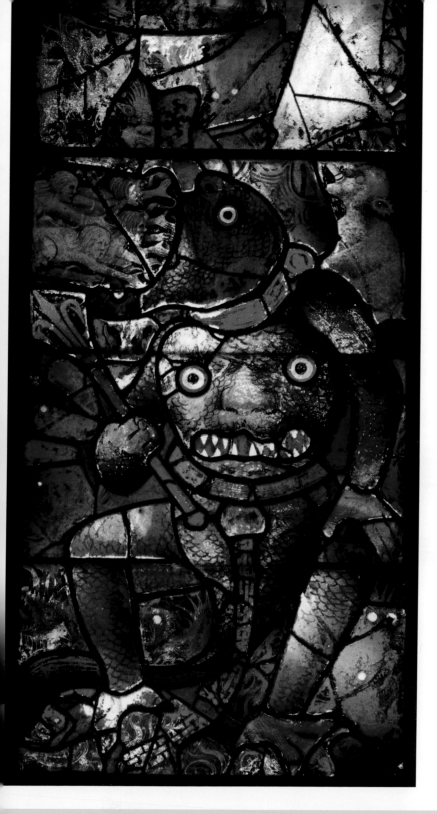

Modern-day images of Satan often look more cartoonish than frightening. To people of the Middle Ages, however, Satan took on many terrifying forms, one of which is depicted in this stained glass window from the 1500s.

During this period, people's image of Satan was not the cartoonish red demon with a tail and a pitchfork that often comes to mind today. According to tradition, Satan could appear in many forms, including as a bright light or a terrifying monster. He could also take human form, such as disguising himself as a false religious leader. Naturally, people tried to shun Satan. Some people avoided eating apples or sneezing, because they thought these actions allowed the devil in. Others sprinkled holy water around their houses, put herbs on their doorsteps, wore necklaces with holy symbols, or avoided areas where witches and devil worshippers were said to appear.

Associating with the Devil

Such efforts did not always succeed. A person who was thought to be possessed by the devil would most likely be brought before a panel of priests. A statement by Tertullian, a writer of the early Christian era, illustrates this:

> Let a person be brought before your [church] tribunals who is plainly under demoniacal possession. The wicked spirit, bidden to speak by the followers of Christ, will as readily make the truthful confession that he is a demon as elsewhere is falsely asserted that he is a god.

> What clearer proof than a work like that? What more trustworthy than such a proof? The simplicity of truth is thus put forth; its own worth sustains it; no ground remains for the least suspicion. Do you say that it is done by magic or some trick of that sort? You will not say anything like that if you have been allowed the use of your ears and eyes.[18]

In general, during the Middle Ages and even into the Renaissance, possessed people were not considered to be at fault; they were seen as blameless, innocent victims. However, this was not true of people who were accused of witchcraft; they were thought to be working with the devil in an unholy alliance that often led to demonic possession of some other unfortunate soul. To combat such horrific acts, authorities enacted strict laws against witchcraft—laws that also carried severe penalties. Witch hunts and trials swept the European continent during these eras. Religious scholar Michael O'Donnell comments, "The records of criminal investigations . . . in which charges of witchcraft or diabolical possession formed a prominent part would fill volumes."[19]

Because most people accused of witchcraft denied their guilt, authorities instituted a wide variety of techniques to exact confessions. The accused were deprived of sleep, beaten, whipped, starved, burned with red-hot iron rods, or worse. Sometimes,

"QUOTE"

"The girl, appearing wild and possessed, ran hither and thither with movements so abrupt and violent that it was difficult to stop her."

—An observer of a possessed nun in 1648.

people were tested by methods other than these direct forms of torture. For example, the accused person was sometimes thrown into a lake or other body of water. It was believed that water could not harm anyone in league with Satan. So floating was proof of sin, and anyone who floated would almost certainly be tortured or put to death. On the other hand, sinking proved innocence—and virtually guaranteed a drowning death. For those found guilty, hanging or burning alive at the stake were common fates. No one knows exactly how many accused witches were executed for being in league with the devil, and estimates vary widely. One source estimates that 80,000 people were killed as witches between 1500 and 1660 in Europe.

The Louviers Possessions

A well-known example of a possession and trial from this period occurred in 1647 at a Catholic convent in Louviers, France. It began when a young nun displayed the classic signs of possession, including convulsions, outrageous sexual behavior, blasphemies, and speaking in unnatural voices. She claimed that two priests caused her torment by forcing her to marry Satan. One of these priests had died by the time the nun made her accusations, but she stated that he continued to control events. Several other nuns then came forward and claimed that the same thing had happened to them.

Like the first nun, they appeared to be possessed. For example, a witness commented on the superhuman strength of one slender young nun. She picked up a marble vase that three normal men could not lift. Using only the tips of her fingers, she turned the vase upside down and threw it on the ground. The witness continued:

> Moreover the girl, appearing wild and possessed, ran hither and thither with movements so abrupt and violent that it was difficult to stop her. One of the clerics present, having caught her by the arm, was surprised to find that it did not prevent the rest of her body from turning over and over as if the arm were fixed to the shoulder merely by a spring. This wholly unnatural performance was carried out some seven or eight times and that with an ease and speed that is difficult to imagine.[20]

"Troubles of Mind"

A vivid description of possession from another era comes from the writings of a seventeenth-century English physician, Richard Napier. Scholars Colin Blakemore and Sheila Jennett write:

> Napier [mentions] patients of his who attributed "troubles of mind," temptations, suicidal thoughts, religious anxieties, and hallucinations all to possession. The more spectacular symptoms of the condition, as established by sixteenth- and seventeenth-century physicians and theologians, included wild physical contortions, superhuman strength, speaking in unknown languages, and reacting adversely to holy words and objects. Possessed individuals often took advantage of their situation to blaspheme [mock religion] or behave in shockingly immoral fashion.

Colin Blakemore and Sheila Jennett, *Oxford Companion to the Body*. Oxford: Oxford University Press, 2001. www.encyclopedia.com.

At the subsequent trial, all of the nuns except one were found to be innocent victims. (The exception, one nun convicted of consorting with Satan, was locked away.) Meanwhile, church authorities exorcised demons from the innocent nuns. The one living priest named by the nun was tortured and burned alive at the stake. The body of the priest who had died before the nun's story was known was dug up and also burned.

The exorcisms and burnings at Louviers were public spectacles. According to some accounts, the screams of the possessed nuns and the tortured priest created a kind of mass hysteria among onlookers, so that the crowd's shouts could be heard far into the countryside.

Demons in Search of Victims

The various sects within Christianity have their own beliefs about demons. Notably, conservative, or fundamentalist, sects within Protestantism generally have more dramatic views on the subject. Speaking broadly, these sects teach that the Bible's references to demons are literal. They also teach that Satan and his demonic followers endlessly search the world, looking for people to torment and destroy. So fundamentalist sects warn that people must be vigilant at all times. Failure to do so, they say, will almost surely result in demonic possession. Brian Connor, a Southern Baptist pastor and exorcist in South Carolina, comments, "Dealing with . . . evil is the single most overlooked component of the biblical mandate."[21]

Fundamentalist clergy, such as Connor, typically advise people to avoid actions or feelings that might make them vulnerable. They often believe this includes sexual feelings (especially homosexual feelings), the occult, unusual religions, drug use, criminal behavior, extreme hostility, physical illness, or listening to certain kinds of music. In extreme cases people who become possessed through such activity might be driven to murder, suicide, arson, or sexual or physical abuse.

The number of fundamentalist churches has grown in recent years in the United States and abroad. As a result, there has been a huge surge of reported possessions and exorcisms. Sociologist Michael W. Cuneo, who studies fundamentalism and exorcisms, comments, "By conservative estimates, there are at least five or six hundred . . . exorcism ministries in operation today, and quite possibly two or three times this many."[22]

Lost Spirits of the Dead

Another of the world's major religions, Judaism, has its own traditions involving possession. As is true in Christianity and other religions, there are many branches within Judaism, each with its own set of beliefs. According to one of these traditions, spirits called dybbuks can possess a person against his or her will. But dybbuks are not demons in the classic sense of the word. Rather, they are the lost spirits of dead people. Gershon Winkler, a rabbi who lives in New Mexico, explains, "[Jews] don't believe in demonic possession. We believe that, on very rare occasions, there can be a possession of a living person by the soul of one who has left the body, but not the world, and they're seeking a body to possess to finish whatever they need to finish."[23] Specifically, dybbuks are the spirits of people who were unable to fulfill their roles in life because of some crisis or obstacle. They can have another chance by inhabiting the body of someone experiencing a similar crisis. The living person has no choice but to fulfill the spirit's destiny.

Some Jewish religious scholars teach that there are many different kinds of spirits, some of them evil. One example appears in the set of writings from the ancient Jewish mystical doctrine

Did You Know?

Tens of thousands of people were tortured and killed in Europe during the Middle Ages because they were suspected of causing others to be possessed by the devil.

called kabbalah. According to this tradition, seven kings rule an army of demons, one king for each day of the week. In some interpretations these demons have wings like angels and can fly anywhere in the world in an instant. Some versions of these teachings hold that dybbuks are unharmed by swords and can fly through fire without harm. Still other traditions say that they can become invisible and reappear in any shape they wish. These disembodied souls can be anywhere, writer and religious scholar Jay Michaelson comments: "They haunt dark places, homes, even the crumbs left on the dinner table."[24]

Spirits of Evil and Mischief

Judaism and Christianity are by no means the only major religions that have traditions regarding spirit possession. All of the world's other major religions have such traditions as well. In many ways these traditions closely resemble those of Christians and Jews.

In the Islamic tradition evil spirits are called jinn (or djinn). Sometimes they are not very evil, only mischievous, but at times they cause serious problems. The writer of a 2009 article in the *Huffington Post* about a Jordanian exorcist comments, "There are tales of good jinn who play with children, and bad ones who create problems with electrical equipment, hide odds and ends throughout the house, or, in some cases, possess people."[25]

According to some sources, evil jinn attack the vulnerable, weak, or mentally ill for any of several reasons. These include a wish to anger Allah (the Islamic name for God) or a lesser emotion such as revenge for an insult. In her book *The Encyclopedia of Demons & Demonology*, Rosemary Ellen Guiley comments, "The djinn especially like to interrupt *Salaah*, or formal prayer; occupy homes and steal the essence

"QUOTE"

"They're seeking a body to possess to finish whatever they need to finish."

—Gershon Winkler, a rabbi, on the Jewish spirits called dybbuks.

of food; and cause mental disturbances and physical illnesses."[26]

Symptoms of possession in the Muslim faith are similar to those identified by other faiths. They include convulsions, speaking in unknown languages, and feeling no pain. An Islamic scholar of the thirteenth and fourteenth centuries, Sheikh al-Islam ibn Taymiyyah, reported one such case. He wrote, "The Jinni enters the one seized by fits and causes him to speak incomprehensible words, unknown to himself; if the one seized by fits is struck a blow sufficient to kill a camel, he does not feel it."[27]

Possession also figures in another of the world's major religions, Buddhism, which is centered in Asia. According to Buddhist tradition, demons were once evil humans. These wicked people have been reborn as spirits who are just as wicked and have the ability to possess living beings.

Young children are especially vulnerable. Before possessing someone, demons can take the form of animals such as cows, lions, foxes, monkeys, horses, dogs, pigs, cats, birds, and snakes. According to a manual by a thirteenth-century Chinese physician, the noises that possessed people make will identify the specific animal spirit inhabiting them.

Possessed by Supernatural Creatures

A belief in the possibility of possession also exists in the Hindu faith, found mainly in India and neighboring Nepal. According to Hindu beliefs, creatures with supernatural powers—called *bhoots*—have the ability to possess living beings. Belief in these spirits dates back to at least 4000 BC. Bhoots are said to be the souls of dead people who met their end in unfortunate circumstances. Perhaps the person committed suicide, or the funeral service was not properly performed. In any case, a bhoot is condemned to wander the earth until it can inhabit another person.

In some cases people ask holy men to place curses on others who threaten or insult them. The holy men then summon spirits to inhabit the target. This possession creates symptoms that are similar to those in other religions, such as screaming, shouting, dancing uncontrollably, and violently shaking one's head. Bhoots also create a number of more serious woes. Scholar Sandeep Singh Chohan states, "Ailments, financial problems, family schisms and even death are viewed as having been caused by some form of supernatural malevolence."[28]

The characteristics of a bhoot can vary, depending on the specifics of a tradition or culture. According to some traditions, bhoots frequently wear white and hide in trees before jumping into someone's body. Sometimes they hide while taking the form of an animal, but if they appear as humans they can be identified by their backward-facing feet. Also, some say bhoots float just above the ground while moving and cast no shadows. Furthermore, it is alleged that the spirits love to swim in milk, so some people avoid drinking it. Other preventive measures include burning a spice called turmeric, sprinkling earth on one's body, and keeping steel or iron objects around.

Shamanistic Possession

Demonic possession was—and in some cases still is—part of daily life for people who live in shamanistic cultures or tribes. In such cases the tribe's holy person, or shaman, can contact the gods and spirits responsible for possession through trances, animal sacrifice, prayers, dancing, and other ritual practices.

Shamanistic religions were once widespread among native tribes in Europe. Examples include the Druids of Ireland and the Sami people of Scandinavia. Overall, however, shamanistic beliefs have now largely disappeared in Europe.

A shaman performs an exorcism in the East African country of Tanzania. Belief in demonic possession can be found in many parts of Africa, where shamans might cast spells that result in possession as well as conduct rituals to exorcise those spirits.

On the other hand, shamanistic cultures that have a belief in spirit possession still thrive in parts of Asia, Africa, the Caribbean, and South America. For example, the Hmong people of Southeast Asia traditionally believe that spirits can appear in dreams and possess a sleeping person. These attacks can be powerful enough to kill the dreamer. People who have recently experienced a serious trauma are thought to be especially vulnerable. And according to a group of Korean shamanistic traditions known as *Muism*, an illness that is caused by possession is called *shin-byung*. The evil spirit can enter a person who has had a frightening or anxiety-producing experience. It creates a number of depression-like symptoms, such as loss of appetite and energy.

Other examples of shamanistic beliefs about possession can be found throughout the Western Hemisphere, from the northern regions of Alaska and Canada to the tip of South America. One example concerns the Miskito people of Central America. They teach that evil spirits can cause a condition that translates as "crazy sickness" and usually affects young women. According to tradition, crazy sickness is highly infectious and can easily spread. Its symptoms include frantic behavior such as tearing off one's clothes and running in fast, erratic ways. Often, victims will run so fast and hard that they fall into dangerous rivers or lakes or collapse from exhaustion. In extreme cases it causes vomiting of bizarre things such as live spiders.

A number of other Latin American shamanistic cultures share a belief in demons that can inhabit a person and create an illness called *susto*. According to this belief, susto causes restlessness, insomnia, listlessness, loss of appetite, and loss of strength. The demon that causes susto enters a person's body when he or she experiences extreme fright or anxiety. Susto can also be triggered if a person angers a nature god. Arthur J. Rubel is an anthropologist who has studied the illness extensively. He writes that it can affect a person who insults the "spirit guardians of the earth, rivers, ponds, forests, or animals."[29]

> ❝QUOTE❞
>
> **"If the one seized by fits is struck a blow sufficient to kill a camel, he does not feel it."**
>
> —An Islamic scholar describing a possessed person.

Spells That Lead to Possession

Shamanistic beliefs in demonic possession can also be found in Africa. Among the many examples are the Zulu and Xhosa people of South Africa. These tribes have a traditional belief in a demonic possession called *amafufunyana*, which results when a shaman casts a spell. Among the symptoms it creates are threatening voices coming from the victim's stomach. Other symptoms include fatigue, loss of appetite, agitation, violent behavior, suicide, uncontrollable anger, and disturbing dreams.

There have been reports that amafufunyana can affect many people at once. According to one source, between 1981 and 1983 over 400 adolescents in Transkei (now part of South Africa) complained of stomach pains, followed by signs of possession. One of these signs was the presence of voices speaking in the Zulu language. This is notable because the Transkei people speak Xhosa. The otherworldly voices were heard when the stomachs of the adolescents were squeezed.

Another example of demonic possession comes from a cult called *zar*. It is found mostly in tribes scattered across northern and northeastern Africa, including parts of Egypt, Somalia, Sudan, and Ethiopia. Anything connected to this belief is called zar. Anthropologist Adeline Masquelier comments, "Zar refers to a type of spirits, the afflictions such spirits may cause, and the rituals aimed at preventing or curing these afflictions."[30]

The majority of possessed people in the zar cult are women. Often, women are also the ones who summon the evil spirit. They can cast spells for a variety of reasons. For example, a woman might bring forth a demon because her husband is considering marrying a second wife (as is common in these tribes), and she wants to keep her husband for herself. In such a case she would cast a spell and cause a demon to possess her rival.

Women who are possessed by zar show a variety of symptoms. These include rude actions such as public smoking, burping, and hiccupping. Victims might also dance wildly, drink alcohol, wear male clothing, threaten men, or speak loudly and crudely. All of these behaviors are highly unusual for the normally polite and dignified women of the region. Some zar traditions hold that afflicted women have an even more varied range of symptoms. According to researchers at Ben-Gurion University of the Negev in Israel, "Possession by Zar is expressed by a wide range of behaviours, such as involuntary movements . . . , mutism [the inability to speak] and incomprehensible language."[31]

Observers have noticed many other symptoms of zar possession. Religious scholar and writer Amsalu Tadesse Geleta notes, "Extreme passiveness, overwhelming fear of evil, extreme confusion, cloudiness of thought and unusual or inappropriate emotional reactions such as laughter, sadness, crying, anger, etc. . . . are characteristics of the demoniacs. [Also] screaming, crying, eating sour leaves, going out naked, and all deeds that are ethically evil are symptoms of a demonized person."[32]

Voodoo Possession

In some cases, as people from Africa have migrated to other parts of the world, their beliefs about demonic possession have spread to other continents. Notably, West African religions were brought to the Western Hemisphere during the slave era. Particularly in the Caribbean island nation of Haiti, these beliefs blended over time with the Catholicism that slave masters practiced. This combination became known as voodoo, which today maintains a rich tradition of spirit possession and exorcism.

Possession in voodoo involves one or another of the religion's thousands of gods and goddesses. Voodoo places a strong

Practitioners of voodoo in the West African country of Benin celebrate the ghosts of their ancestors through dance and various rituals. These spirits are thought to visit earth by possessing living people at certain times of year.

emphasis on honoring these deities, as well as on honoring the spirits of the dead. Paying tribute to these gods, goddesses, and spirits of the dead is crucial, in large part because they play major roles in guiding and controlling the living. Possession by an evil spirit is, of course, not something to be sought; but in voodoo, possession is often considered a good thing. This is because coming into contact with certain spirits can bring good fortune, love, and prosperity.

As a result, elaborate ceremonies are regularly held for this purpose, typically involving drumming, dancing, and animal sacrifice. In a major part of these ceremonies, people willingly invite spirits to possess them. The spirit can then control the individual and offer advice, cures for illnesses, and predictions for the future. Frenzied dancing and uncontrollable movements, such as extreme trembling, usually accompany the possession. When the spirit leaves, the person is exhausted and remembers nothing about what happened.

An Array of Beliefs and Traditions

Voodoo and other traditions that include belief in possession are as diverse as they are geographically scattered, and there is virtually no part of the globe or period of history that does not have some such tradition. While some cultures' ways of regarding possession resemble each other closely, others are very different from each other. Overall, they represent the tremendous variety and vitality of religious beliefs around the world—especially the belief that otherworldly spirits can possess the living.

CHAPTER 3

Exorcists: Chasing the Demons

Ted (not his real name) was an airline pilot who led a normal life in most ways, but he had also been deeply depressed for years. His depression contributed to the ruin of his marriage and to thoughts of suicide. Psychiatric treatment did not help. A friend suggested that he might be possessed by a demon and referred Ted to a husband-and-wife team who perform evangelical exorcisms. (Evangelicalism is a longstanding but rapidly growing movement within the branch of Christianity called Protestantism. Simply put, one of its distinctive characteristics is a strong belief in spreading its message among non-evangelicals.) Finally, Ted found the relief he was seeking. He met with the couple in their living room, and "Pastor Frank," as the husband is known, prayed. Ted immediately felt something. He recalls, "It was like a twitching—you can feel something moving in your leg or stomach. You know something's in there. You can feel it moving up through your body and out through your mouth, your ears, your eyes."[33]

Exorcisms like this one are so low-key that they could be mistaken for counseling or prayer sessions. Cathi Nowlen, who oversees a ministry in South Carolina, comments, "It's not a big deal to get demons out. We don't shout at demons—they're not deaf."[34]

However, this is not always the case. For example, Gabriele Nanni, a Catholic priest in Italy, says that during an exorcism he can sometimes actually see violent evidence of demons within a person's body. He comments, "Sometimes you can see it, under the skin, in the abdomen and stomach area, an unexpected thing lifting up and down, like a snake or frog. The ensnared person is as though tied by an umbilical cord to the devil."[35]

In Previous Centuries

Modern Catholic exorcisms such as the ones Nanni performs are vastly different from those of previous times. For one thing, exorcism rituals centuries ago were usually public spectacles, witnessed by large and rowdy crowds. Exorcists of long ago also used a number of methods that today seem bizarre. For example, priests in the Middle Ages sometimes shaved a cross in the possessed person's hair. They might also tie down the afflicted person near a church, reasoning that Satan could not bear to hear religious services. Sometimes more drastic measures were needed. Psychology professors Dennis Coon and John O. Mitterer comment, "For the fortunate, exorcism was a [nonviolent] religious ritual. More often, physical torture was used to make the body an inhospitable place for the devil to reside."[36]

This torture typically included such techniques as starvation, beating, bloodletting, and submersion in icy water. But the most extreme measure was trepanning. In trepanning, a doctor drills a hole in the afflicted person's skull to release demons. Amazingly, some people survived this procedure.

Modern Catholic Exorcisms

In contrast to these rituals of old, Catholic exorcisms today typically stress privacy. Generally, the only people in the room are the afflicted person, the exorcist and his assistants, and perhaps a few close family members. This ensures that confidentiality can be maintained. As one priest, John A. Hardon, comments, "The last thing the Church wants is to give the devil publicity."[37]

If the exorcist expects violence, he might begin by removing potentially dangerous items and, if needed, restraining the afflicted person on a bed or chair. Violence during an exorcism is rare in Catholicism, however. It has been estimated that only 2 or 3 out of every 100 Catholic exorcisms involve dramatic events. (The estimates of how many exorcisms the Catholic Church does each year vary widely, from a few to several hundred.)

The rite itself usually follows a well-established set of procedures. The exorcist holds up holy objects, such as a cross, lays his hands on the afflicted person, and recites prayers to God and commands to Satan. Reciting the prayers and commands takes only about an hour, although the ritual can last much longer if removing the demon seems to be especially difficult. It frequently lasts for several hours, and multiple sessions are sometimes needed. One of the most important parts of a typical Catholic exorcism is a commandment to leave, directed at the demon. The exorcist does this by reciting these words (or variations on them):

I command you, unclean spirit, whoever you are, along with all your minions [servants] now attacking this servant of God, by the mysteries of the incarnation, passion, resurrection, and ascension of our Lord Jesus Christ, by the descent of the Holy Spirit, by the coming of our Lord for judgment, that you tell me by some sign your name, and the day and hour of your departure.

I command you, moreover, to obey me to the letter, I who am a minister of God despite my unworthiness; nor shall you be emboldened to harm in any way this creature of God, or the bystanders, or any of their possessions. [38]

The exorcism rituals are contained in a book called the *Roman Ritual*, originally written in 1614. The rituals were unchanged until 1999, when the document was revised to reflect more modern ideas. Notably, the new regulations formally allow priests to consult medical experts. Also, an exorcist has freedom to deviate somewhat from the standard ritual. For example, he is allowed to conduct the ceremony in his own language (as opposed to Latin, the church's official language). He can also use different prayers or change the order of events. A Canadian exorcist, François Dermine, comments, "I never follow the Ritual exactly the way it is organized in the book. . . . It comes as it comes, depending on the reaction of the person. I remember one time with one person, as soon as I started to pray, the person went under possession and in that case there is not really the time to read the Bible and stuff like that. You have to pray."[39]

"The last thing the Church wants is to give the devil publicity."

—John A. Hardon, a priest, on why Catholic exorcisms are kept private.

Although exorcisms are done infrequently in modern times, trained exorcists can still be found in the Roman Catholic Church. Father Carmine de Filippis, shown on the steps of his church in Rome, has been an exorcist since 1983.

The process of a Catholic exorcism does not end when the formal ritual ends. In the aftermath of a completed exorcism, the afflicted person will likely need to be nursed. Psychiatry professors Jean Goodwin, Sally Hill, and Reina Attias comment, "Careful watch is kept after the exorcism, and physical/medical care is given to the possessed person who may be quite weak."[40]

Investigation

In previous centuries many priests were quick to perform exorcisms on people believed to be possessed. For the modern

Catholic Church, however, an exorcism is a last resort. First there is a lengthy investigation to see whether an alleged possession is, in fact, caused by mental illness—or, in very rare cases, fraud. The church first assigns special investigators. They examine evidence and testimony, oversee medical and psychiatric exams, and conduct background checks on everyone connected to the case.

The investigators look for the three basic signs that indicate possession: superhuman strength, the ability to understand unknown languages, and the knowledge of things that the person could not possibly know. But they also look for other signs, such as a rejection of church teachings or a fear of holy objects. Typically, people from a variety of fields support the investigators. The church's regulations state: "The exorcist will decide [a case] with experts in medical and psychiatric science."[41] A typical support team might include a clinical psychologist, a psychiatrist, and a physician.

Estimates vary considerably on the percentage of cases that are considered to be true possessions. The late Corrado Balducci, longtime exorcist of the Archdiocese of Rome, suggested that only 5 or 6 out of every 1,000 people who seek help are really possessed. Most suffer from mental illness that can be addressed with psychiatric help and medication. In an article on new methods of training Catholic exorcists, *Baltimore Sun* reporter Arthur Hirsch comments, "In the great majority of cases . . . church officials say, what the person really needs is help of a less dramatic nature: a doctor, a therapist or simple pastoral counseling."[42]

If church investigators decide that a case is one of possession, not mental illness, a church leader authorizes a final step: an exorcism conducted by a specially trained priest. No one knows exactly how many trained exorcists there are in the world; one expert estimates 150 to 300 worldwide. Perhaps one measure is that

the International Association of Exorcists, which was founded in 1993, has about 200 members.

Commanding Spirits to Leave

Other branches of Christianity typically also perform exorcisms as a last resort, although in many cases these sects have very different ideas about exorcisms. For example, some sects within the Anglican Church (Church of England) teach that restless souls can cause possessions. These souls are in Purgatory, a state in which they are made ready to enter heaven. In this case a mass for the dead may be enough to comfort them and help them move on.

On some occasions, Christian exorcisms are performed not on people but on places, such as a home. Such a possession might involve inexplicable voices coming from the house, or objects flying around inside it. If a building is deemed to have demons living in it, an exorcist might be called in. One such exorcist is Barry May, an Anglican priest and former police chaplain in Australia. May says that he performs about 10 exorcisms a year, most of them on homes inhabited by spirits. May points out that his rituals are quite aggressive:

> I have a prayer that is very commanding and very demanding. You don't go into a house and say: "Excuse me Mr Ghost, you can go now". It's very, very serious stuff.
>
> Demons can exhibit in some pretty nasty manifestations too, so you don't take it lightly.
>
> By the end of it I'm sweating, profusely. It takes a lot out of me. It's almost like you've got a fever.

You've got to do what you do and it drains me at the time because you put so much effort and energy into this. You're not playing games. This is deadly serious.[43]

A Forceful Expulsion

Some conservative Christian denominations stage exorcisms not as quiet, private affairs, but as highly public and often boisterous events. Some are routinely shown on television or the Internet. And some are mass rituals in which large groups of people are exorcised at once. One of the most famous of these exorcists is Bob Larson. Larson is a flamboyant figure who is a regular guest on media broadcasts around the world. Calling himself the "Real Exorcist," he claims to have conducted more than 10,000 successful rituals.

A typical Larson-led exorcism involves a large audience that sees several men holding the allegedly possessed person. Larson holds a Bible or cross in one hand and speaks in a gentle, hypnotic voice to the person at first, explaining what he is going to do. But the event quickly grows more dramatic. The afflicted person tries to escape the grip of Larson's helpers. He or she typically convulses and speaks in a strange, hostile voice. Larson's actions match this, escalating to high-energy prayers to God and commands to Satan. This is answered by the person speaking in strange and equally violent voices. Larson also touches the afflicted person, perhaps by placing his hand on the person's forehead or placing a Bible or cross on the person's chest.

As the ritual ends, believers say, the devil is forcefully expelled, typically through the person's mouth. The exorcist puts his hand on the afflicted person's forehead and says a final prayer before

hugging the person. This approach is reflected in Larson's public statements, such as: "Spiritual fighters never negotiate with the devil. This is war, not a negotiating table."[44]

Healing the Soul

Many exorcists in other religions are far less belligerent. For instance, Judaism has its own methods of exorcising dybbuks. In ancient times these methods included burning herbs, giving poisonous root extracts to the afflicted person, and dunking him or her in water. But, as with most sects in Christianity, Jewish exorcisms are rare. The majority of rabbis (Jewish religious leaders) feel that most alleged possessions are actually caused by mental illness. If, however, someone is deemed to be genuinely possessed, the exorcism ritual is usually held in a synagogue. The rabbi begins by purifying himself, typically with water and oil. He also plays his shofar (ram's horn trumpet). This serves to loosen the possessing demon's grip on the afflicted person. The rabbi then begins the ritual, which focuses on prayers from the Old Testament and other sacred books, songs, and discussion.

One goal of the conversation with the dybbuk is to learn whether it is genuinely evil or just a lost spirit. The rabbi asks its name and tries to understand why it has inhabited the afflicted person. This will then help the rabbi see what is troubling the dybbuk, and what can be done to help it—and thus allow it to leave. In this way the ceremony becomes an opportunity for both the demon and the possessed person to heal whatever is afflicting them. Rather than forcing dybbuks away, Jewish exorcisms typically focus on allowing them to leave. Gershon Winkler comments, "We don't drive anything out of anybody. What we want to do is to heal the soul that's possessing and heal the person."[45]

An important part of the process is a debate with the spirit.

This give-and-take allows the two sides to understand each other and to reach a compromise. Goodwin, Hill, and Attias comment, "Negotiation, bargaining, and persuading is often used, as well as limit-setting. . . . This bargaining process can go on for some time, with the spirit offering other alternatives [to leaving]; it may pretend to have left [or] promise to be kind to the possessed person. Finally, the spirit agrees to leave on its own, given certain conditions."[46]

If the dybbuk refuses to compromise, the rabbi and his colleagues typically threaten the spirit. They do this by repeating special chants, each time more forcefully. This verbal aggression is almost always enough. However, a few rare cases have been recorded when beatings were necessary to drive a dybbuk away. When an exorcism is successful, according to tradition, the dybbuk leaves the afflicted person's body through a finger or toe. Rabbi Geoffrey Dennis comments, "The primary sign of a successful exorcism [is] a bloody fingernail or toenail."[47] This is the point through which the dybbuk entered the body in the first place.

Battling the Deceiver

In many ways Islamic exorcisms closely resemble those of Judaism and Christianity. For one thing, they are rare, since the cause is usually determined to be mental illness. Islamic religious leaders sometimes do see instances of genuine possession, and in those cases exorcisms might be authorized. The Islamic exorcism ceremony is called a *ruqya*. *Ruqyas* sometimes involve aggression—even, in some extreme and very rare cases, to the point of beating the person. Some Islamic scholars have compared a strong exorcist to a general at the head of a battle. Religious scholar Shawana A. Aziz comments, "For, surely this type of treatment [an exorcism] is, in fact, war . . . and the warrior will not be able to defeat his enemy unless he fulfills two conditions: that his weapon is sound and sharp, and that his arm is strong."[48]

The prayers used in an exorcism come from Islam's holy book, the Koran. The sprinkling of holy water is also important. In this case it comes from the Zamzam Well in Mecca, Islam's most sacred city. Islamic exorcists also engage the demon in conversation over what is troubling it. During this conversation, the exorcist tries to reach a compromise with the spirit. For example, the spirit might agree to move to an isolated place, such as an abandoned

Evangelical minister Bob Larson (pictured) claims to have conducted more than 10,000 successful exorcisms. Convulsions and dramatic outbursts are not uncommon in these ceremonies, which are often performed before large groups.

building or a barren patch of countryside, in exchange for a promise that it will be left alone.

However, the imam (religious leader) must be careful when talking to the spirit. This is because the spirit may try to trick the exorcist. In fact, some Islamic scholars assert that the statements of demons should never be regarded as true. According to Rosemary Ellen Guiley, "[The] djinn must be rebuked, warned, shamed, and cursed in the same ways permitted against human beings. . . . It is permissible for exorcists to listen to what the possessing djinn have to say, but it is forbidden to believe them, for they are deceivers."[49]

Compassion and Flames

Across Asia, a number of religions have strong traditions regarding possession and exorcism. The most widespread of these is Buddhism. Within Buddhism there are many different exorcism practices. For instance, some authorize a significant amount of aggression, including slapping or shouting at a possessed person to dislodge a spirit. Exorcisms might also involve forced fasting or repeatedly dunking the afflicted person in ice-cold water.

However, these practices are exceptions. In most Buddhist sects exorcism rituals emphasize meditation, prayer, and compassion toward the spirit. In this way, exorcism becomes a method for letting a misguided spirit (and the possessed person) eliminate negative thoughts and achieve a higher state. Religious scholar Shen Shi'an comments, "Buddhist exorcism does not aim to kill, trap, hurt, or chase away harmful unseen beings. . . . This [attitude] is similar to trying to reform abusive human criminals."[50]

In Tibet, a mostly Buddhist nation, an exorcism might begin with offers of food and other objects to the Buddha. A lama (re-

A Long-Distance Exorcism

The world's first attempt at an exorcism by Skype was done in the Jewish tradition. According to news reports, in 2010 a Jewish man in Brazil started having convulsions, during which he spoke in three languages he did not know. Even though his lips did not move, his abdomen moved while the voices came out of him. They said things like, "The end is close" and "I sense many sins." Afterward the man remembered nothing about these fits.

A rabbi in Israel agreed to try a long-distance exorcism. He decided to go ahead with it despite the opinions of other rabbis, who felt an exorcist had to be in the same room with the afflicted person. He arranged to perform an exorcism on the Brazilian man long distance, using Skype. Unfortunately, the ritual was not a success. The Brazilian man had to arrange to go to Israel to get rid of his demon.

Quoted in "Rav Batzri Attempts Dybbuk Removal via DybbukVision," *Matzav*, December 24, 2009. http://matzav.com.

ligious leader) creates a special design called a mandala, using sand to represent the fleeting nature of life. Then the food is thrown onto a fire, drawing the demon into the flames. Sometimes, the lama lures the demon into a bowl and then throws it on the fire. In some Tibetan sects, religious leaders "hurt" the demon by throwing stones and other objects at symbols of demons. Sometimes whole villages dance for days to drive the spirits out.

In Japan Buddhist exorcisms are rare. A typical ritual might involve a temple's chief priest and his assistant reciting certain prayers, called mantras, and burning incense. The priest also carries a *shakujo*—a long wooden stick threaded with metal rings that make noise to drive demons away. In some Japanese religions, such as the Mahikari cult (a relatively new sect that combines Buddhism with a variety of shamanistic faiths), an exorcism may also include another ritual, according to anthropology professor Thomas A. Green. He writes, "Often, the exorcism ritual involves a laying on of hands. In the Japanese Mahikari cult, the hands are held up, palms out, and thought to exert a curing force on the subject. Here, as in many other belief systems, if the subject becomes physically sick and vomits, a purification is believed to be taking place."[51]

Ash and Incense

In Hinduism, as in Buddhism, the specifics of exorcism differ from region to region. For example, some Hindu traditions ban

> ## "QUOTE"
>
> "For, surely this type of treatment [an exorcism] is, in fact, war . . . and the warrior will not be able to defeat his enemy unless he fulfills two conditions: that his weapon is sound and sharp, and that his arm is strong."
>
> —Islamic scholar Shawana A. Aziz.

exorcism. In others, exorcists perform rituals to drive demons out. The rituals typically include such actions as burning incense and holding leaves from a neem tree while conducting the ceremony. (These leaves are widely held to have cleansing and healing properties.) Prayers from holy texts called the *Vedas* are also recited. Sometimes, the exorcist will ritually beat the afflicted person with a broom or slipper.

Other forms of exorcisms in Hinduism can involve keeping pictures of certain gods and sprinkling water from holy rivers around the person's house. And in some cases the exorcist blows sacred ash and rubs pig dung on the afflicted person. Still another method is to offer food, especially sweets, to the spirit. All of these methods are designed to drive spirits out or keep them away.

Another culture from India, the Dravidian people in the southern part of that country, have their own traditions. A Western scholar, Wilber Theodore Elmore, illustrates by quoting a witness to a mass exorcism at a Dravidian temple in 1912:

> As the priests pass from one [worshipper] to another, some one of the patients will begin to sway backward and forward, and round and round in a counter clockwise motion. Then others take up the same motion, and soon all are swaying round and round. . . .
>
> Sometimes the swaying is gentle and dreamy, and at other times it is accompanied with loud cries, and at times with reproaches [accusations] directed at the priests. The afflicted persons often work themselves into a fury and twist violently around, striking the earth with the palms of their hands.[52]

Elephants, Dances, Drums, and Songs

In the mountainous nation of Nepal, which is in large part Hindu, another striking example of an exorcism took place in 2001. It demonstrates how Hindu exorcisms are generally calm, healing rituals, not violent events. This gentle ceremony is especially notable because it followed a shocking incident: the assassination of Nepal's king. It was conducted to cleanse the nation of any remaining trace of evil spirits, which in turn allowed the king's spirit to depart in peace.

One part of this ritual involved a priest eating small bits of 84 sacred dishes. These dishes contained small bits of animal bone marrow. (This is normally forbidden, since a significant number of Hindus are vegetarians.) After that, the priest put on the king's robe and crown, as well as heavy black eyeglasses similar to those worn by the ruler. He then climbed onto an elaborately decorated elephant. Some of the king's personal possessions and other items were strapped to the elephant's back. These included television sets, bedding, and baskets of food. Finally, the elephant was led out of the valley, symbolically driving out the killer's evil spirit and allowing the king's soul to rest forever.

Like Hinduism and Buddhism, shamanistic exorcisms from around the world can have many variations. Typically, however, they share such characteristics as dancing, drumming, and singing that put both the shaman and the afflicted person into trances. One such example is a healing ceremony still performed by Navajo tribes in the American Southwest. This ceremony, called the Enemy Way, typically lasts for three days. Members of the possessed person's family help the shaman (sometimes called a medicine man).

The ritual includes singing, the use of items such as corn pol-

"The primary sign of a successful exorcism [is] a bloody fingernail or toenail."

—Geoffrey Dennis, a rabbi, noting the traditional way a dybbuk leaves a possessed person.

len, juniper branches, ashes, and smoke from burning sage leaves. Another important object is a personal item belonging to the afflicted person. The medicine man may also give the person a drink that causes vomiting, expelling the evil spirit. Typically, the exorcist also ritually stabs the evil spirit with a "sword" consisting of a raven's beak attached to a stick.

A Zar Ritual

Another example of a shamanistic exorcism, that of the zar cult, is one of many such rituals found in Africa. For this ceremony, the possessed woman dresses in white, often in clothing reserved for men. As a sign of purification, she wears intricate makeup and is heavily perfumed, as are the guests.

A female shaman called a *kodia* leads the ritual. Women are her primary helpers. (Men do help out, usually by gathering material for offerings to the gods or drumming during the ceremony.) The kodia puts the afflicted woman in a trance and negotiates with the spirit. Dancing, singing, and drumming are also part of the ritual. Dance expert Karol Harding describes one zar ceremony:

> Each woman moved to the pulse of the drum. . . . The sick woman's movement increased in intensity and speed, her eyes half closed, she appeared totally oblivious of her surroundings, abandoning herself completely to the dance.
>
> Her movements flowed freely from the inside out . . . gaining strength and speed as she came full circle around the imposing altar to where the helpers were . . . till finally, she threw her arms up and was about to fall, but the Kodia guided her to the floor.[53]

A zar exorcism is expensive. The guests and the afflicted woman's husband all contribute money, with the husband providing most of it. This serves as the kodia's salary. Expenses are also high because another part of the ceremony involves making offerings of food. (According to one source, zar spirits are especially fond of coffee.) The expenses mount if valuable animals such as chickens, sheep, or camels are sacrificed.

If the demon is satisfied by the ceremony, it will leave. However, the possessed person will continue to be at risk. He or she must therefore keep away from dirt or unclean objects and avoid negative emotions. Furthermore, sometimes an exorcism is not successful, which means that several attempts will be needed—at extra cost.

A Violent Cure

Another example from Africa comes from tribes in Angola, on the continent's west coast. These cultures believe that children are especially vulnerable to demons called *kindoki*. The cure can be very violent. Sometimes a shaman will rub pepper in the eyes of an afflicted child, cut him or her with a knife, or threaten drowning to make the demon leave.

Immigrants from Angola sometimes carry their belief in kindoki, and the need for casting them out, to other countries. For example, a woman named Sita Kisanga went on trial in England in 2005 for taking part in an exorcism that severely abused a child. Over several weeks, the girl was cut with a knife, beaten with a belt and shoe, and had chili powder rubbed in her eyes. Kisanga told a reporter, "Kindoki is something you have to be scared of because in our culture kindoki can kill you and destroy your life completely. Kindoki can make you barren. Sometimes kindoki can ruin your chances of staying in this country [England]. The authorities will arrest you and deport you and kindoki can be part of it."[54]

Some shamanistic exorcisms are so violent that they are life-threatening. For example, in 2009 a Haitian immigrant in New York City, Marie Lauradin, was arrested for conducting a near-fatal exorcism. She sprayed rum on the floor of her home around her six-year-old daughter Frantzcia, whom she believed was possessed, then poured more rum on the girl's head and lit the child on fire.

Frantzcia lived, although she was permanently scarred. Her mother was convicted of assault and endangering the welfare of a child. Frantzcia's grandmother was convicted of reckless endangerment, because she did nothing while her granddaughter burned and did not take her to the hospital right away.

But such cases are exceptions that anger many followers of voodoo. They point out that voodoo is overwhelmingly a positive force for cultural identity. *New York Times* reporter Dan Bilefsky comments about violent ceremonies, "[Mainstream] practitioners say they were aberrant [abnormal] acts perpetrated by ignorant people who were abusing the religion."[55]

No matter whether its basis is in voodoo or another religion or culture, belief in exorcism is still widespread across much of the world. The world's major religions, and the many others that existed or still exist, all consider the ritual important. So, although possession is a rare occurrence, to members of these faiths it is a serious phenomenon that requires a serious answer: exorcism.

CHAPTER 4

Is Possession Real?

C learly, many people believe that possessions really occur. There are forces in the world, they say, that cannot be recognized through normal human senses. Some of these forces, these observers contend, are spirits that do no harm. Some are positive entities that clearly do good things. Others, however, may be demons that actively possess and harm people. On the other hand, many experts are not convinced about these supernatural events. Specifically, these skeptics question whether possession is genuine. And if not, they ask, is exorcism real?

The majority of skeptics assert that there are rational explanations for the bizarre and terrifying behavior of allegedly possessed people. To them, belief in possession is just superstition, ignorance, or gullibility. For example, some demonic possessions supposedly give their victims superhuman strength. Skeptics assert that this can be explained by the fact that humans often have enormous strength in times of stress or crisis because adrenaline is pumping through their bodies.

Speaking in unknown languages, meanwhile, might simply be

a case of an exorcist not understanding the language or not recognizing that it is a real language and therefore assuming that it is nothing more than gibberish. Furthermore, skeptics argue, vulnerable people can subconsciously convince themselves that they are possessed. And sometimes other people sway them toward such beliefs, on purpose or not. Vincenzo Mastronardi, a professor of psychology and a Catholic, adds, "From what I have observed in thirty-five years as a clinical psychologist, exorcism is really a kind of hypnosis. It is both autohypnosis and hypnosis by a priest who does it without knowing. And then they think that what happens is the action of the devil. When it ceases, the devil has gone away."[56]

Brain Disorders

Like Mastronardi, many skeptics who question possession are professionals who deal with mental health and brain disorders. This group includes psychiatrists, psychologists, therapists, physicians, and neurologists. Today, most of these mental health professionals suspect that no single disorder is to blame. Instead, the cause could be one of several illnesses or some combination of them. All of them produce various symptoms that could easily be mistaken for possession—especially in times past when knowledge of the body and the brain were limited.

One such condition is epilepsy. Epilepsy is not a mental illness. It is a neurological disorder. With epilepsy, the brain sends out faulty electrical signals that cause convulsions or seizures. The person with epilepsy usually has no memory of these afterward. Sometimes epilepsy takes milder forms, such as short spells of staring at nothing, as if the afflicted person is in a trance. Furthermore,

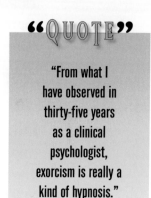

"QUOTE"

"From what I have observed in thirty-five years as a clinical psychologist, exorcism is really a kind of hypnosis."

—Vincenzo Mastronardi, an Italian professor of psychology and a faithful Catholic.

Many people
believe that
possession and
exorcisms are
really caused by
mental illness or
medical conditions.

some people with epilepsy report unusual sensations just before a seizure. These include tingling skin, smelling odors that are not there, or experiencing sudden emotional changes.

Another neurological disorder that might create possession-like symptoms is Tourette's syndrome (TS). TS causes people to have frequent, uncontrollable, and repeated physical movements and outbursts of speech. The symptoms of TS can be fairly minor. For example, they might be no more serious than having a facial tic or making occasional grunting noises. Although TS symptoms are rarely severe, in more serious cases they can include jumping uncontrollably, shouting obscenities, or striking out violently.

The other disorders that might cause possession-like symptoms are mental illnesses. The most common of these is schizophrenia, a disabling illness that affects about 1 percent of Americans. Schizophrenics frequently have hallucinations (seeing things that are not there) or delusions (strong false beliefs, such as hearing voices that other people cannot hear). Schizophrenics may also believe that other people can read their minds or control their thoughts, or are plotting to harm them. Conversely, some schizophrenics think they can understand and control the thoughts of others. Furthermore, schizophrenics may sometimes speak nonsense or sit for hours without moving or speaking.

Dissociative Identity Disorder

Another rare condition that might be mistaken for possession is dissociative identity disorder (DID). (This condition was once called multiple personality disorder.) Sufferers of DID take on more than one identity. Research indicates that past histories of extreme trauma, such as mental, physical, or sexual abuse, are behind the vast majority of DID cases. Many professionals suspect that DID occurs when a person's mind separates itself from

A woman's face reveals strong emotions as she undergoes an exorcism in Mexico. Is possession real, as those who have experienced it say it is? Or is it the result of superstition, ignorance, or illness, as skeptics believe? Proof of either view is elusive.

the terror of trauma. The normal, healthy self is unable to handle the memories, so it invents new personalities that are stronger or that have no connection to the trauma. DID is rare. When it does happen, it most frequently affects people who experienced their trauma as children.

The multiple personalities "live" inside the person and can emerge at unexpected moments, especially in times of stress. Usually, they come out one at a time, and the emerging personality takes control. Cases of people with as many as 100 separate personalities have been reported, although research indicates that the average is 10. These personalities typically have very different characteristics.

For example, each one can have a distinct gender, age, set of behaviors, language, ethnic origin, or level of intelligence. They can even appear to have different physical characteristics. For example, they can differ in their allergic reactions, right- or left-handedness, physical disability, or eyesight. In addition to multiple personalities, DID can cause other symptoms, such as trances, during which the afflicted people ignore everything around them. Sufferers might also act in self-destructive ways, such as cutting themselves. And they sometimes feel that they have out-of-body experiences, during which it seems as though their spirits leave their bodies.

Psychiatrists as Believers

Although the majority of mental health professionals say they do not believe in possession, a few of them are not sure. For example, psychiatrist and author M. Scott Peck studied and wrote extensively about the concept of evil and the devil. At first, Peck agreed with the majority of his psychiatric colleagues in doubting the possibility of possession. Peck did research to find ways to explain his patients' conditions using established psychiatric techniques, but he was unable to find satisfying answers. He later commented, "I was a scientist, and it didn't seem to me I should conclude there was no devil until I examined the evidence. It occurred to me if I could see one good old-fashioned case of possession, that might change my mind. I did not think that I would see one, but if you believe that something doesn't exist, you can walk right over it without seeing it."[57]

Some psychiatrists feel that exorcisms are not real but

"I was a scientist, and it didn't seem to me I should conclude there was no devil until I examined the evidence."

—Psychiatrist and possession researcher M. Scott Peck.

that they still serve a purpose. They regard the rituals as valuable tools for helping mentally ill people come to terms with their problems. In this view, if mentally ill people convince themselves that they are possessed, an exorcism might help them symbolically cast out their imagined demons. Matt Baglio comments:

> For many years, the scientific and medical community scorned the idea that a person could be "healed" through prayer or ritualistic ceremonies like exorcism. Today, however, the ability of certain healing rituals to offer genuine relief is no longer disputed—numerous anthropologists have documented that people have recovered from problems varying from depression, addictive behavior, or anxiety to even more severe ailments, including life-threatening diseases, through such ceremonies.[58]

Concerns About Vulnerable People

Mental health professionals are not the only skeptics. Many—but not all—religious leaders are also concerned that naive people may mistake mental illness for possession. One is Bob DeWaay, the former pastor of a Christian organization called the Twin City Fellowship in Minneapolis, Minnesota. DeWaay used to perform exorcisms regularly, but he stopped because he did not think they significantly helped anyone. Since that time, DeWaay states, he has seen virtually no cases and came to suspect that the symptoms he saw occurred because he unconsciously suggested them. He comments, "There were people apparently going about a normal life, but if they came into the deliverance room to get this ministry they would get these demonic manifestations. They weren't really changing, they were just getting convinced that whatever happened in life and whatever personal shortcomings they might have had a demonic cause."[59]

Most other authorities in the world's major religions agree with this theory. This is why these religions conduct thorough investigations before authorizing exorcisms. Jorge Arturo Medina Estévez, a cardinal in the Catholic Church, comments, "Exorcism is one thing, and psychoanalysis is another. If the exorcist has any doubt about the mental health of the possessed, he should consult an expert. . . . It often happens that simple people confuse somatic [physical or mental] problems with diabolical influence, but not everything can be attributed to the devil."[60]

Was Anneliese Michel Mentally Ill?

Many mental health professionals have studied the famous case of Anneliese Michel, both while she was alive and since her death. A number have concluded that she suffered from mental illness, pointing out that many of Anneliese's symptoms were those typically found in patients with psychiatric problems.

Doctors diagnosed Anneliese with epilepsy and schizophrenia. However, recently a number of professionals have suggested that she could have suffered from DID as well, a condition that was not recognized at the time. The doctors who examined Anneliese tried to treat her, but the medication they gave her was not effective. As a result, Anneliese and her parents rejected their advice and were convinced that she was indeed possessed. Many other people around her believed this as well—and many still do. Anthropologist Phillips Stevens comments, "Despite the tangible, natural explanation of the woman's affliction and the mass media's nationwide presentation of it, many believers have persisted in seeing the episode as a supernatural phenomenon. . . . She was certain of the reality of Satan and his command of demons that could possess people."[61]

Danger

If people have symptoms like Anneliese's but are unwilling to seek (or continue with) medical help, they may try to solve the problem through exorcism. However, this course, on rare occasions, can lead to disaster. Journalist Tracy Wilkinson, in her book *The Vatican's Exorcists*, comments, "Failure to discern serious illness, and instead attributing it to the work of the devil, has led to death in a small number of exorcisms over the years."[62]

For example, in 2009 a married couple in the American South were charged with murder in the death of their six-year-old daughter. The adults were arrested after police found them wandering aimlessly in Fulton County, Georgia. They were naked, even though the weather was freezing cold, and they had two other children with them. Police later found the girl's body in a motel room where the adults had been living. She had been strangled, stabbed, beaten, and covered in pages torn from a Bible. According to a CBS News report, there was no direct evidence that an exorcism had taken place. However, a police spokesperson, John Quigley, told reporters that the parents said that God had told them to conduct a ritual that "had something to do with 'undemonizing' the child."[63]

In another chilling example, an exorcism was performed in

> " QUOTE "
>
> "For many years, the scientific and medical community scorned the idea that a person could be 'healed' through prayer or ritualistic ceremonies like exorcism. Today, however, the ability of certain healing rituals to offer genuine relief is no longer disputed."
>
> —Writer Matt Baglio.

No Proof

Michael W. Cuneo, a professor of sociology, witnessed many exorcisms during the course of doing research for his book *American Exorcism: Expelling Demons in the Land of Plenty*. He saw many troubled people in various forms of apparent possession, but he also asserted that nothing proved the existence of demons. He commented:

> So what did I see? Some of the people who showed up for exorcisms seemed deeply troubled, some mildly troubled, and some hardly troubled at all. The symptoms they complained of—the addictions and compulsions, the violent mood swings, the blurred self-identities, the disturbing visions and somatic sensations—all this seemed to me fully explainable in social, cultural, medical, and psychological terms.
>
> There seemed to be no compelling need, no need whatsoever, to bring demons into the equation. The same with the antics I sometimes witnessed while the exorcisms were actually taking place, the flailing and slithering, the shrieking and moaning, the grimacing and growling—none of this, insofar as I could tell, suggested the presence of demons.

Michael W. Cuneo, *American Exorcism: Expelling Demons in the Land of Plenty*. New York: Doubleday, 2000, p. 274.

2005 on a young nun who was part of an isolated religious community in Romania. This nun showed typical signs of schizophrenia, but others around her thought she was possessed. A priest and several nuns tried to cast out the demons by tying her to a cross, pushing a towel into her mouth, and leaving her alone without food or water. Three days later, she died of dehydration, exhaustion, and a lack of oxygen.

Government authorities in Romania shut down the community and arrested the priest and four of the nuns. At the time, the priest defended his actions. He told reporters, "You can't take the Devil out of people with pills."[64] However, he and the nuns were convicted of manslaughter. The nuns received sentences ranging from five to eight years in prison, and the priest was sentenced to 14 years.

Still another deadly exorcism, dating from 2011, concerned a man and a monk in the southern Japanese city of Kumamoto. They belonged to a tiny, breakaway sect of Buddhism. The two tried to perform an exorcism on the man's 13-year-old daughter. According to the British newspaper the *Telegraph*, "Reports said the girl's parents had turned to the monk after the youngster had suffered several years of mental and physical ill health that doctors had not been able to resolve. The monk . . . said that the girl was possessed by an evil spirit."[65]

So the father and the exorcist tied the girl to a chair as a pump poured water onto her face from a special underground well. The girl's father also held her down. Meanwhile, the monk chanted prayers. They later testified that they had performed this ritual on the girl many times in the past. The girl's mother called an am-

> ❝QUOTE❞
>
> "Exorcism is one thing, and psychoanalysis is another. . . . Not everything can be attributed to the devil."
> — Jorge Arturo Medina Estévez, a Catholic cardinal.

bulance after her daughter lost consciousness but it was too late, and the girl drowned.

A Historical Case of Fraud

Another danger posed by people who are seemingly possessed, as well as people who claim to be exorcists, is that they might be perpetrators of outright fraud—that is, nothing more than fakers. There are many such cases from the present day, but the phenomenon is rooted in the past. One historical example concerns a sixteenth-century Frenchwoman named Marthe Brossier.

When she was 25, Brossier suddenly began showing signs of demonic possession. First of all, she behaved in unusual ways. She cut her hair and wore men's clothing—extraordinary actions for that time and place. Furthermore, she was unmarried—another abnormal condition for a woman her age. And Brossier showed classic signs of possession. She periodically screamed and contorted her body into grotesque shapes. In addition, she attacked her friend Anne Chevion, claiming that Chevion was a witch who had cast a spell on her.

Brossier and her family thought they could make money from exploiting her condition. They traveled up and down the Loire Valley region around their village, asking local priests to exorcise her demons in public. These spectacles drew large crowds of curious people, and the Brossier family charged people money to attend an exorcism. There likely was another reason for Brossier's fraud besides simply making money. She was Catholic and fanatically opposed to breakaway sects of Protestants. In particular, she wanted to discredit one of these sects, the Huguenots. Perhaps not surprisingly, many of the devil's blasphemous pronouncements issuing from her mouth condemned the Huguenots.

Brossier's career as a possessed person came to an end when

she encountered a Catholic bishop in the town of Angers who proved that Brossier was a fraud. He brought water near her and told her it was holy water. She violently rejected it, which was a typical sign of possession. However, the water was just plain water. The bishop then told her he was going to recite a prayer. He spoke in Latin, the official language of the Catholic Church (which Brossier did not understand). The young woman again reacted violently, as if the demon within her was resisting a command to leave. Then the bishop revealed that the Latin he had recited had nothing to do with religion. It was simply a quotation from an ancient poem by the Roman poet Virgil.

Brossier fled to Paris and tried to revive interest in her alleged demonic possession. However, doctors and religious scholars there also determined that she was simply a fraud, with no signs of demonic possession. As a result, the French king, Henry IV, imprisoned her—and her symptoms went away.

Modern Fraud Cases

Examples of similar frauds continue to this day. However, cases like Brossier's are unusual. Not many people nowadays falsely claim to be possessed. Much more common are cases in which fake exorcists are nothing more than con artists. Their mission is to take advantage of gullible people for personal gain.

Typically, these phony exorcists portray themselves as spiritual healers with special powers. They dupe people who are desperate to be rid of evil spirits. In such cases the phony healers claim to have occult or paranormal powers that let them communicate with spirits. They are thus able to take advantage of people, in sharp contrast to exorcists who are authorized by recognized religions. Legitimate exorcists from these religions do not accept money for their services.

An example of an outright fraud occurred in 2011 in the African nation of Zimbabwe. A man there was given an 18-year prison sentence for raping a woman while pretending to exorcise "bad things" that were in her stomach. This was an instance of a man duping a naive woman by pretending to be a genuine healer. A judge in the case commented, "There is no doubt that the accused ... hid behind his position as a spiritual healer/prophet."[66]

Orthodox Romanian nuns mourn the death of a 23-year-old member of their order, who died in 2005 during a three-day exorcism ritual. The nuns and the priest who conducted the ritual were convicted of manslaughter and imprisoned.

Money-Stealing Schemes

Another example of fraud concerns Bridgette Evans, a fortune-teller in Broward County, Florida. She was arrested in 2011 on a charge of fraud. Her crime was being the leader of a scheme to steal thousands of dollars from people by claiming that she could cast out their evil spirits. Evans and her team of criminals told their clients that evil spirits were responsible for their bad financial luck, illnesses, and romantic failures. Evans claimed that for a fee she could end these problems. The clients paid the fees, but their problems did not stop. Evans did not just fail to do what she claimed she could do. She had promised to return the money when the spirits were gone. She never did. According to police, Evans and her crew stole about $60,000 before they were caught.

A third example comes from Japan. According to the British Broadcasting Corporation, a Japanese man, Shunichi Miyazaki, and eight accomplices were accused in 1983 of taking large sums of money to perform exorcism rites in various cities around Japan. Police investigators said that the crew approached likely targets in train stations and other public places.

The criminals were dressed in tennis clothes and carried rackets or violin cases. This made them seem more credible to their potential clients. The con artists then told their targets such things as, "Your back is possessed by the spirit of a dead woman and she has attached strings to your neck," or "The spirit of a dead man with severed legs is [clinging] to your waist."[67] The criminals then offered to exorcise these spirits through prayer for fees ranging from about $250 to $8,500. Those who agreed, mainly women in their twenties and thirties, were taken to what the con men called a chapel in the mountains, or to hotel rooms, where the criminals performed prayers and a variety of invented rituals.

After their arrests, the team was convicted of fraud, having taken an estimated $350,000 from their victims. Miyazaki denied that he had done anything wrong. He stated, "When I was a high school student, I nearly drowned. After the incident I came to have psychic power. I didn't mean to cheat them and it is not a fraud."[68]

Are Other Exorcists Frauds?

In addition to frauds such as these, a number of skeptics have questioned the actions of a small percentage of Christian evangelists. These critics charge that a few fraudulent ministers prey on vulnerable people, guaranteeing that they will be rid of alleged demons in exchange for money. The need for caution is critical, according to critics like psychiatrist Richard E. Gallagher, who states:

> One has only to turn on a television to witness obvious abuses—for instance, televangelists dunning their audience for cash as they conduct exhibitionist [flamboyant] ceremonies before large assemblies of the overly credulous [naive]. . . .
>
> Some of the individuals who fall prey to these groups are largely conscious of their tendency to exaggerate or distort; others are fully self-deluded and without any insight or self-knowledge. They can become fully caught up in their disorders and their supposed need for "spiritual" rather than psychiatric therapy . . . and may too readily be led to believe that they are being attacked by the devil or evil spirits.[69]

Perhaps the most prominent minister who has been criticized over the years is Bob Larson, the man who calls himself the "Real Exorcist." Skeptics point out that Larson charges admission to his public exorcisms; he also charges for DVDs and other items he sells at these events. Furthermore, many critics, including *World* (a Christian magazine) and a number of former Larson employees, have alleged that he hires people to sit in the audience and these people pretend to be possessed so that it appears Larson is exorcising them.

Public Fascination Is Ongoing

The world has always been fascinated with possession and exorcisms, and this interest has been increasing in recent years. No one is certain why this is so, although it is likely a combination of things. Among these are the spectacular growth of evangelical churches and their emphasis on exorcism. Also, the Internet has made it much easier for interested people to communicate with each other.

Adding to the spike of interest is popular culture's ongoing obsession with the topic. The most recent surge of interest began with *The Exorcist*, a 1971 novel that was made into a wildly popular movie in 1973. Since then there have been many other movies on the subject, including several sequels to *The Exorcist* and films such as *Dominion, The Exorcism of Emily Rose, The Last Exorcism, Constantine*, and *The Rite*.

"Science can't explain everything."
—Italian psychiatrist Salvatore di Salvo.

All of these films are fiction, but a number of serious nonfiction books, films, articles, and academic studies have also explored the subject. Despite all this attention, there has been no definitive proof thus far about either the reality or the falsehood of demonic possessions and exorcisms. Perhaps the truth will never be known. On the other hand, believers may someday prove that demons do exist—or skeptics may prove that they do not.

In the meantime, there is still much in the world that cannot be explained logically or scientifically. Salvatore di Salvo, an Italian psychiatrist, comments, "Science can't explain everything."[70] Until definite answers are found, the search for the truth will continue.

NOTES

Introduction: Inhabited by Spirits

1. Jody Bower, "The Loa Mounts: Physical, Religious, Cultural, and Psychological Aspects of Possession," e-mail message to author, November 29, 2011.
2. Matt Baglio, *The Rite*. New York: Doubleday, 2009, p. 40.
3. Quoted in Gilbert Cruz, "The Story of a Modern-Day Exorcist," *Time*, March 16, 2009. www.time.com.
4. Cruz, "The Story of a Modern-Day Exorcist."
5. Paul Burnell, "Exorcisms on the Rise," Catholic Education Resource Center, 2000. www.catholiceducation.org.

Chapter 1: In the Grip of Demons: The Possessed

6. Quoted in Chasing the Frog.com, "Questioning the Story," 2012. www.chasingthefrog.com.
7. Quoted in Chasing the Frog.com, "Questioning the Story."
8. Quoted in Traugott Konstantin Oesterreich, *Possession and Exorcism: Among Primitive Races, in Antiquity, the Middle Ages, and Modern Times*. Cedar Knolls, NJ: Wehman Brothers, 1974, p. 7.
9. Quoted in Michael W. Cuneo, *American Exorcism*. New York: Doubleday, 2000, p. 45.
10. Adolf Rodewyk, *Possessed by Satan*. Garden City, NY: Doubleday, 1979, p. 140.
11. Quoted in Albert C. Gaw et al. "The Clinical Characteristics of Possession Disorder Among 20 Chinese Patients in the Hebei Province of China," *Psychiatric Services*, March 1, 1998. http://ps.psychiatryonline.org.
12. Quoted in Alexia Amvrazi, "The Eyes Have It: The Evil Eye in Greece," Athens Survival Guide. www.athensguide.com.

Chapter 2: Possessions Throughout History and Across Cultures

13. Colin Blakemore and Sheila Jennett, *Oxford Companion to the Body*. Oxford: Oxford University Press, 2001. www.encyclopedia.com.
14. Anne Sutherland, "Cross-Cultural Medicine: A Decade Later," *Western Journal of Medicine*, September 1992. www.ncbi.nlm.nih.gov.
15. John A. Hardon, "What Are Possession and Obsession by the Devil?," Real Presence Association. www.therealpresence.org.
16. Darren Oldridge, "Demon Possession in Elizabethan England," *English Historical Review*, September 2007. http://ehr.oxfordjournals.org.
17. Quoted in Roger Baker, *Binding the Devil*. New York: Hawthorn, 1974, p. 13.
18. Quoted in Hardon, "What Are Possession and Obsession by the Devil?"
19. Michael O'Donnell, "Demonical Possession," *Catholic Encyclopedia*. New York: Robert Appleton, 1911. www.newadvent.org.
20. Quoted in Lewis Spence, *An Encyclopaedia of Occultism*. North Chelmsford, MA: Courier Dover, 2003, p. 302.
21. Quoted in Ed Vulliamy, "Americans Plagued by New Demons," *Observer* (UK), October 7. 2000. www.guardian.co.uk.
22. Quoted in Oliver Libaw, "Exorcism Thriving in U.S., Say Experts," ABC News.com, September 11, 2001. http://abcnews.go.com.
23. Quoted in Jeff Belanger, "Dybbuk—Spiritual

Possession and Jewish Folklore," Ghostvillage
.com, November 29, 2003. www.ghostvillage
.com.

24. Jay Michaelson, "Demons, Dybbuks, Ghosts,
& Golems," MyJewishLearning.com. www.my
jewishlearning.com.

25. *Huffington Post*, "Jordanian Exorcist Scares
Jinn Out of Patients," May 31, 2009. www.huff
ingtonpost.com.

26. Rosemary Ellen Guiley, *The Encyclopedia of
Demons & Demonology*. New York: Check-
mark, 2009, p. 78.

27. Quoted in Shawana A. Aziz, "Do Souls of the
Dead Return Back to the World?," AHYA.org.
www.ahya.org.

28. Sandeep Singh Chohan, "The Phenomenon of
Possession and Exorcism in North India and
Amongst the Punjabi Diaspora in Wolverhamp-
ton," master's thesis, University of Wolver-
hampton, August, 2008. http://wlv.openreposi
tory.com.

29. Quoted in Peter J. Brown, ed., "The Epidemiol-
ogy of a Folk Illness: Susto in Hispanic America,"
*Understanding and Applying Medical Anthro-
pology*. Mountain View, CA: Mayfield, 1998.

30. Quoted in Islamweb.us, "What Is the ZAR in Islam?," May 29, 2011. http://islamweb.us.

31. E. Witztum, N. Grisaru, and D. Budowski, "The
'Zar' Possession Syndrome Among Ethiopian
Immigrants to Israel: Cultural and Clinical As-
pects," *British Journal of Medical Psychology*,
September 1996. www.ncbi.nlm.nih.gov.

32. Amsalu Tadesse Geleta, "Case Study: Demoni-
zation and the Practice of Exorcism in Ethiopian
Churches," *Lissan*, September 2009. http://lis
sanonline.com.

Chapter 3: Exorcists: Chasing the Demons

33. Quoted in Ben Whitford, "Evangelical Exorcists
Do Battle with Devils," *Daily Camera* Boulder
(CO), April 9, 2005. www.rickross.com/refer
ence/exorcism/exorcism26.html.

34. Quoted in Whitford, "Evangelical Exorcists Do
Battle with Devils."

35. Quoted in Tracy Wilkinson, *The Vatican's Exorcists*. New York: Warner Books, 2007, pp.
65–66.

36. Dennis Coon and John O. Mitterer, *Psychology:
A Journey*. Florence, KY: Cengage Learning,
2010, p. 511.

37. Hardon, "What Are Possession and Obsession
by the Devil?"

38. Quoted in Catholic Doors Ministry, "Rite of Exorcism," 2007. www.catholicdoors.com.

39. Quoted in Baglio, *The Rite*, p. 75.

40. Jean Goodwin, Sally Hill, and Reina Attias,
"Historical and Folk Techniques of Exorcism:
Applications to the Treatment of Dissociative
Disorders," *Dissociation*, June 1990. https://
scholarsbank.uoregon.edu.

41. Quoted in BBC News, "Vatican Issues New Exorcism Rules," January 27, 1999. http://news
.bbc.co.uk.

42. Arthur Hirsch, "New Interest in Exorcism Rites
Comes to Baltimore," *Baltimore (MD) Sun*, January 10, 2011. http://articles.baltimoresun.com.

43. Quoted in Nicole Fox, "Former Police Chaplain
Now WA's 'Ghost Buster' Doing Exorcisms,"
PerthNow (Perth, Australia), April 22, 2010.
www.news.com.au.

44. Bob Larson, "Bob Larson's Latest Book: Demon
Proofing Prayers," www.boblarson.org.

45. Quoted in Belanger, "Dybbuk—Spiritual Possession and Jewish Folklore."

46. Goodwin et al. "Historical and Folk Techniques
of Exorcism: Applications to the Treatment of
Dissociative Disorders."

47. Geoffrey Dennis, "Jewish Exorcism," MyJewish
Learning. www.myjewishlearning.com.

48. Aziz, "Do Souls of the Dead Return Back to the
World?"

49. Guiley, *The Encyclopedia of Demons & Demonology*, p. 78.

50. Shen Shi'an, "How Not to Break 'Rule #1,'" The
Buddhist Channel, March 17, 2008. www.bud
dhistchannel.tv.

51. Thomas A. Green, *Folklore: An Encyclopedia of Beliefs, Customs, Tales, Music, and Art*, vol. 1, Santa Barbara, CA: ABC-CLIO, 1998, p. 268.

52. Quoted in W.T. Elmore, *Dravidian Gods in Modern Hinduism.* PhD dissertation, 1915 Reprint, Whitefish, MT: Kessinger.

53. Karol Harding, "The Zar Revisited," *Crescent Moon*, July/August 1996, pp. 9–10.

54. Quoted in James Westhead, "Abuser Speaks of Witch Belief," BBC News, June 3, 2005. http://news.bbc.co.uk.

55. Dan Bilefsky, "Voodoo, an Anchor, Rises Again," *New York Times*, April 8, 2011. www.nytimes.com.

Chapter 4: Is Possession Real?

56. Quoted in Wilkinson, *The Vatican's Exorcists*, p. 153.

57. Quoted in Laura Sheahen, "'The Patient Is the Exorcist': Interview with M. Scott Peck," Beliefnet, January 2005. www.beliefnet.com.

58. Baglio, *The Rite*, pp. 200–201.

59. Quoted in Cruz, "The Story of a Modern-Day Exorcist."

60. Quoted in Irene Carson, "The Exorcism Ritual—How to Perform It and the Risks Involved," *Christian Daily World*, October 18, 2010.

http://christiandailyworld.com.

61. Phillips Stevens, "Children, Witches, Demons, and Cultural Reality," *Free Inquiry*, Spring 1997. http://search.proquest.com.ezproxy.spl.org.

62. Wilkinson, *The Vatican's Exorcists*, pp. 4–5.

63. Quoted in CBS News, "Exorcism Suspected in Child Death," February 11, 2009. www.cbsnews.com.

64. Quoted in Craig S. Smith, "A Casualty on Romania's Road Back from Atheism," *New York Times*, July 3, 2005. www.nytimes.com.

65. *Telegraph* (UK), "Teenage Girl Dies in Japan 'Exorcism,'" September 27, 2011. www.telegraph.co.uk.

66. Quoted in Charles Laiton, "Self-Proclaimed Prophet Jailed 18 Years," *NewsDay* (Zimbabwe), August 16, 2011. www.newsday.co.zw.

67. Quoted in BBC News, "Japanese 'Psychic' Arrested for Exorcism Fraud," January 22, 2003. http://news.bbc.co.uk.

68. Quoted in BBC News, "Japanese 'Psychic' Arrested for Exorcism Fraud."

69. Richard E. Gallagher, "Among the Many Counterfeits," *New Oxford Review*, March 2008. www.newoxfordreview.org.

70. Quoted in Wilkinson, *The Vatican's Exorcists*, p. 5.

FOR FURTHER RESEARCH

Books

Jane P. Davidson, *Early Modern Supernatural: The Dark Side of European Culture, 1400–1700*. Santa Barbara, CA: Praeger, 2012.

Susan R. Gregson, *Investigating Demons, Possessions, and Exorcisms*. North Mankato, MN: Capstone, 2011.

Rosemary Ellen Guiley, *Spirit Communications*. New York: Chelsea House, 2009.

William K. Kay and Robin Parry, eds., *Exorcism and Deliverance: Multi-disciplinary Perspectives*. Milton Keynes, England: Paternoster, 2011.

Kristi Lew, *Monsters, Beasts, and Demons in America*. New York: Rosen, 2011.

Brad Steiger, *Real Monsters, Gruesome Critters, and Beasts from the Darkside*. Canton, MI: Visible Ink, 2010.

Websites

Catholic Encyclopedia, **Exorcism** (www.newadvent.org/cathen/05709a.htm). This site supplies a discussion of the Catholic stance on exorcism, from the *Catholic Encyclopedia*.

HowStuffWorks, How Exorcism Works (http://science.howstuffworks.com/science-vs-myth/afterlife/exorcism.htm). These pages provide a good introduction to the subject of exorcism.

Islam Universe, Exorcism (www.islam-universe.com/Exorcism.html). A discussion of exorcism from an Islamic perspective.

Jewish Encyclopedia.com, Exorcism (http://jewishencyclopedia.com/articles/5942-exorcism). This site has details on Jewish traditions about demonic exorcism.

Religious Tolerance.org, Demonic Possession, Oppression & Exorcism: Conservative Protestant Beliefs and Practices (www.religioustolerance.org/chr_exor4.htm). This site provides information about Protestant attitudes on possessions and exorcism.

Index

E

G

W

Weaver, Johann, 32
Wilkinson, Tracy, 75
Winkler, Gershon, 39, 40, 57
witchcraft, 35

Z

zar (African cult), 45–46
    exorcism in, 65–66
Zeno of Verona, 25

Possessions and Exorcisms

Picture Credits

Cover: Thinkstock/iStockphoto

AP Images: 59

© Keith Dannemiller/Corbis: 71

© Historical Picture Archive/Corbis: 9

© Rainer Holtz/Corbis: 28

© Alex Masi/Corbis: 53

© Caroline Penn/Corbis: 47

Photofest Digital Pictures: 23

© Proimage/epa/Corbis: 80

Thinkstock/iStockphoto: 16

© Nik Wheeler/Corbis: 43

Window depicting Satan (stained glass), English School, (16th century) /
St. Mary's Church, Fairford, Gloucestershire, UK / The Bridgeman
Art Library: 33

ABOUT THE AUTHOR

Adam Woog has written many books for adults, young adults, and children. He lives in Seattle, Washington, with his wife. They have an adult daughter.